SCARRED
Marked
Book 2

EMMY LOU HAYES

Published by Blushing Books
An Imprint of
ABCD Graphics and Design, Inc.
A Virginia Corporation
977 Seminole Trail #233
Charlottesville, VA 22901

Scarred
Emmy Lou Hayes

eBook ISBN: 978-1-63954-449-3
Print ISBN: 978-1-63954-450-9

Cover Art by ABCD Graphics & Design

Prologue

I WATCH *her drive into the darkness. Headed away from me. I'm losing my chance. I've lost my hope in this. I follow her down the mountain. I will not give up just yet. I will prove to her that she loves me and needs to return. She will be mine. Mine and mine alone.*

I have waited hundreds of years in the shadow of others. Gone unrecognized for my commitment. Been given so little reward, only to watch them get everything they have ever wanted. I won't stand for it any longer. I refuse to be left here in the darkness and not given what I so wholly deserve.

They will pay for what they have done to me, she will pay for what she has done to me. For the slight and rejection of me.

Chapter 1

EMILY

"Tell me about it?" I lean on my elbow propped on the bed next to Theo.

"About what?" He rolls onto his side, his eyes meeting mine.

"About being a wolf, what's it like?" I approach the question cautiously, not even sure how to ask it at all.

"Freeing, but also like being caged. I spent nearly three hundred years as a wolf living with the vampires, Alaric, and Blake. It felt like being in a cage. I was trapped in that form, but after a hundred years or so, I got used to it. Got used to being a wolf, more wolf than man." His voice is even, his tone low, he closes his eyes as he rolls on his back and I know he is remembering it, that time in his life. It was not so long ago. Less than a month since they escaped the coven.

"Do you miss it? Living as a wolf, I mean?" Theo sighs at my question.

"Some days, but most days, no. I like the freedom of

being able to decide when I want to take on that form and when I don't. Being forced into it for so many years wore on me." He rolls toward me again and kisses me on the cheek.

I smile over at this man, this werewolf. I can't fathom that I am actually here with him. Waiting for my sister to give birth to his niece who is not only part werewolf, but also part vampire. Theo's brother, Alaric is a werewolf who was bitten by a vampire over three hundred years ago.

Sasha fell in love with the man who saved her from a coven of vampires who were after her to breed her and bring on a new line of day walking vampires. Or so they have all told me since I arrived here, and they started filling me in on all the details. I don't know how much of it I believe and how much I think that maybe they're all having mental break-downs of some sort.

"Theo?" I look into his eyes, mine moving back and forth as I look over his face.

"Hmm?" He smiles a grin at me that if I let it could break my heart.

"Will you show me, again?" I ask him this out of curios-ity. I saw him shift once, we were in the park, Sasha and me. A wolf approached us and then shifted into the man lying in the bed next to me. I fainted.

I believe what they tell me to an extent, but to another, I still don't believe my own mind and what I saw that day. I still need proof. I need to see it again with my own eyes. I need to confirm that I'm not crazy, that this is all really happening, and these men are who they say they are.

"Emily, if you're ready, then I will gladly show you who I am, all of me." Theo smiles at me and it warms my insides.

Theo stands from the bed and crosses to the middle of the room, I squeeze my eyes closed, not sure if I'm ready for what he is about to show me.

"You're going to have to open your eyes, Em," he tells me and I open one slowly, looking in his direction.

When he shifts then, he takes on the form of the beautiful wolf I saw in the park that day with Sasha. Landing on all fours in front of me on the floor he stalks toward me slowly.

"Theo?" I tilt my head to the side examining the beast in front of me. His eyes are the same.

This wolf standing before me is the man who was just lying in bed next to me. It is really him. He is truly a werewolf. As Theo closes the final gap between us, he rests his head on the edge of the bed and looks up at me, his eyes filled with sadness and doubt at what I can only assume, is my failure to accept him for what he is.

Reaching out slowly I rest my hand on top of his head, his fur is soft, thick, and smooth under my fingertips. I lace my fingers through it and scratch behind his ear. He tilts his head, and the moment feels incredibly intimate for some reason.

I cannot accept him in his human form as a man I am willing to drop my walls for and let into my heart like he has asked me to do. But here, now, with him as his wolf I am more than willing to coax him into bed with me, curl up with my head on his side and fall asleep holding him.

It isn't fair. I know it isn't. But I pat the bed anyway. Theo climbs up next to me and I curl up next to him, resting my head on his side. Softly, I begin to tell him about myself, about my past, losing our parents, everything. It pours out of me, and I feel comfortable with him in this moment, baring myself to him, my life, my emotions.

After a long while I grow quiet and sit in the silence, just enjoying my time with him.

"Theo?" I ask him, and he shifts beneath me, lifting his head and looking back in my direction.

"I don't know. I simply don't know if I can do this." My honesty cuts through him like a knife and I feel his entire body tense under me.

Theo presses his nose to my hand, then buries it under my palm and lifts my hand on top of his head, nuzzling me.

I know he is telling me it is all right. That he will give me the time and the space I need to make this decision. He will allow me to hold him at arms-length, pulling him in closer to me as I push him away again and again as I have the weeks I have been here.

I close my eyes and slowly drift off, toying with the fur on top of his head as I do.

Theo

Emily falls asleep with her head on my side, and I lay awake for hours, just enjoying the sensation of the weight of her head on me. The feeling of having her so close to me. I gave her exactly what she wanted, what she asked for, but I fear it has only driven the wedge between us further into the gap she has placed there.

Slowly I move on the bed, slipping out from under Emily, when I climb down from it I look back over my shoulder at her. Shifting back into my human form, I undress and cross the room toward her again.

It takes everything I have not to wake her, not to slip my hands over her body and worship her the way I so badly want to. Instead, I gently lift her, shifting her on the bed and laying her gently back on the pillows, then climb in beside her and pull her against my body.

"Theo," she whispers my name softly in her sleep. I smile

down at this woman who has so captured me. Has completely taken me, heart, and soul, and then pushed me away.

Kissing her gently on the forehead I pull her to me and wrap her in my arms. I will find a way to make her mine. Find a way to break down the walls she has put up between us. I know it has only been a short time, but I knew the moment I saw her in the park with Sasha that she was my mate.

Knew then that I was meant to make her mine and claim her. I will do just that, no matter what it takes, no matter what the cost. I will wait for her for as long as I have to, but Emily will be mine in the end. I have waited too long, hundreds of years to find her. I refuse to let her slip through my grasp now.

Emily

When I wake Theo is lying next to me, stretched out with his arm over my stomach, in his human form again. The soft light of the sun is filtering in through the windows and I look over at him, at this man who is asking me for so much but expecting so little in return.

I make the decision then, I cannot stay. I cannot let him in and risk losing everything to someone who could so completely destroy me. I will have to tell him, have to explain that I am leaving as soon as Sasha's baby is born. I need to go home, back to my life, back to the existence that I am so familiar with, where it is safe for me and my heart.

Chapter 2

EMILY

I left him. I left Theo the day after Alexandria was born. I couldn't stay. I couldn't let myself fall in love with a werewolf. That may be how Sasha wants to live her life, but I don't. I want to go home and be normal. If there is even such a thing.

As I make my way down the mountain road, I think back to our night together. The night I let my guard down and let him slip into my heart. Into me.

It was weeks ago now, I stayed at their home while we waited for the birth of my sister's baby. Surrounded by the magic of the place and the love my sister and Alaric had for each other. I got swept up in the moment and thought I could stay there with him, forever.

I know now that I cannot. That I must return home to my life and reality. The memories and emotions will fade in time, just as they have a way of doing. For now, I get lost in them. Letting them wrap their arms around me in the darkness and imagine myself back with him. Back with Theo.

"Emily." He calls my name as I stand by the back door.

When I turn and look at him, the deep glow of his eyes reflecting the flames of the fire he stands beside warms my heart and I know what he is asking me in this moment.

"Theo." I hold my hand out to him as he crosses the patio toward me.

As he reaches me, he lifts me into his arms, and I wrap my legs around his waist. Letting him carry me into the house and down the hall to his bed.

When he tosses me back onto the bed, I giggle.

"God, that sound is music to my ears, Em," Theo tells me as he climbs onto the bed on top of me.

His arms framing my face, knees pinning my hips to the bedspread.

"I have thought about this moment since the first time I saw you in the park. When I spotted you, I knew I needed to make you mine, to bury myself inside you, and hear you call my name as I did."

"Theo," I put my hands on his chest, wanting to put some space between us, his words stirring something inside me. Making this all too real. Making it all mean too much. "It isn't like that—" I try to tell him. He cuts me off with his kiss and stars explode in my vision when our lips meet.

"Shut up woman," he growls out the words at me as he kisses over my jaw and down my neck. "Just let me make love to you."

I nod softly in the dark room, my eyes adjusting to the low light coming in through the windows. I see him move on top of me and lower himself to my abdomen, moving my shirt out of the way and kissing my belly, my hips, down over my skin, setting it on fire as he goes.

When he reaches the waistband of my jeans, he quickly undoes the button and then lowers the zipper slowly. Looking up at me through hooded eyes, the devotion I see in them startles me and I again want to put a stop to this. Want to stop myself from falling over the precipice into something I cannot take back.

I don't. I let him go on. My need for him in this moment is stronger than my desire to set boundaries. I lift my hips off the bed as he curls his fingers under the edge of my jeans and slowly pulls them down over my hips, then my thighs. Exposing me to him. The small triangle of fabric covering me, all that is left between us.

Raising my arms over my head, I allow him to slip my shirt off next. My breasts pushed up to my chin by my bra. I lay back on the bed in nothing but my undergarments. Staring up into the eyes of a man who looks as if he would worship me given the chance.

"Theo," I start.

"Emily." he drops his mouth to mine again. Hungry and hard. When he kisses me this way I cannot think straight. I cannot protest.

Sitting back on his knees between my legs I watch him strip off his own shirt and get lost in seeing the muscles bunch and smooth with his movement. This man is one who I could let myself worship, if I could only open my heart to him.

Lowering his body back over mine he grinds himself against me, the bulge between his legs pushing against the soft fabric of my thong, pushing me to the edge. As he slips his hand down between our bodies he slides under the edge of the fabric and finds my pussy. Long, expert fingers trace circles over my clit, dipping inside me as he goes.

I pant, getting lost in the moment then. Throwing all caution to the wind and allowing him to do with me what he will.

His other hand goes to his jeans button, he frees himself quickly. Pants pushed down to his hips. I watch as his dick bobs in the moonlight. When he pushes down on the base of himself leveling the head of it with my waiting pussy, I arch my back and lift myself off the bed toward him.

Pinning me down by my hip with his hand he uses the other to tease me with the head of his cock. When Theo pulls back from me, I watch *as he slips a condom packet from his back pocket. Opening it, he sheaths himself. When he goes back to teasing me, I moan out his name.*

"Theo, mmm. Don't stop."

"Never," he agrees. Then continues to rub himself up and down my slit.

Pushing ever so slightly into me he slides back out, again and again, each time giving me more of himself. More of his length buried inside me.

A blaring horn brings me back to the present from my memories and I jerk the wheel pulling my car back into my lane.

"Shit, Em. Get it together," I scold myself, tightening my grip on the steering wheel.

I press on the brake pedal, slowing myself and change lanes. Tucking in behind the car I nearly ran off the road moments before.

The rest of my drive home is uneventful. I keep my attention on the road and avoid daydreaming about Theo. I have to get home tonight, so I drive straight through. I work tomorrow and can't afford to take any more time off. The month I spent with Sasha, Alaric, and Theo has taken a major hit on my savings, and bills won't wait any longer.

By the time I pull up outside of my house the sun has long risen, and my eyes burn from lack of sleep. I lug my belongings up the driveway behind me and collapse onto the sofa the second I pass through the front door. I think I fall asleep before my head even hits the throw pillow on the couch.

I wake to the sound of my alarm going off. My body is sore from sleeping on the cramped couch in my living room. I roll off it onto the floor and adjust my shirt. Glancing down at my watch, I have just enough time to change and run a brush through my hair before I have to leave for my shift at the bar.

When I rush out the front door to my car, barely making it out of the house in time for my shift, I stumble over the bouquet of flowers on the front porch.

"What the hell?" I scoff as I hear them crunch under my foot.

Scooping them up off the sidewalk I take them with me to the car. Toss them into the passenger seat and head out of the driveway.

She tramples over the flowers I laid for her on the porch and doesn't even give me a passing glance as she heads toward her car.

I stand shadowed in the bushes, waiting. Watching. Willing her to look in my direction. Nothing, I'm not given a second thought. Neither is my gift as she tosses it, forgotten, onto the passenger seat of her car and speeds off into the night.

Theo

I sit at the end of the bar, watching Emily work. I have been here since shortly after seven when she arrived for her shift, and she has yet to notice me. The other bartender at this end of the bar, has been tending to me and my steady flow of drinks.

I observe her carefully, watching the way her body moves under her silk blouse, the way it brushes against her skin when she leans forward over the bar, laughing at something one of her customers just said.

It makes me hard, seeing her this way. Lit up and in her element. Thinking about the way my skin brushed against her as I rode her in my bed not so long ago. Watching the curve of her ass in her jeans as she turns and bends to pick up a napkin that just fluttered to the ground at her feet. I picture her perfect, naked body beneath mine. Remembering the way she tasted as I lower my mouth to the rim of my glass and toss back the last of my whiskey. This isn't going to work. Just sitting here and watching her.

I am clearly already being forgotten by her. Tossed aside like a week-old bouquet of flowers, in the trashcan, wilted and forgotten. Sighing, I raise my hand to the bartender and order another round. One more I tell myself, one more and I'll have the balls to march down there and tell her she is coming back with me.

She has been gone for twenty-four hours and already my bed is cold and lonely without her. The long drive here behind her was one I wouldn't wish on any man. Watching the love of your life disappear over the horizon again and again, knowing that you're chasing her down as she runs from you and the life you could lead together.

One more round, then I'll have the courage to tell her how I feel and take her home with me.

Chapter 3

EMILY

When he sits down in front of me, I catch a glimpse of him from the corner of my eye. He looks familiar. But I can't quite put my finger on where I have seen this man before. I set the glass I was washing down in the sink, and steady myself before I look up.

I turn to look at him head on now and he smiles at me. A wicked grin that sets me on edge and raises the hairs on the back of my neck.

"Hey, beautiful girl," he greets me and I return his greeting with a nod and a small smile of my own.

"What can I get you?" I ask, pulling a clean glass from under the counter.

"Whiskey sour." He winks at me.

"Coming right up." I turn around and face the back of the bar, our rail liquors lining the wall, and select the ones I need for his order.

As I set the glass down on the bar in front of him, he

reaches out and grazes the back of my hand with his fingertips. Brushing it off as him reaching for his drink, I go back to work and tend to the rest of my customers.

The stranger nurses his drink for the next hour. As I check back in on him periodically, he just nods. Continuing to sip at his whiskey.

"You're not really a talker, are you?" I ask as I wipe down the bar. It is nearing the end of my shift and the majority of the patrons have gone for the night, the few left, here and there, are closing out their tabs and heading home.

"I'm more of an observer," he tells me. "I like to get a good lay of the land. Study my surroundings. Plan out my moves."

I raise my eyebrows at him, scrunching up my face.

"All right. Well, we are about to shut down for the night. Can I get you anything else before I close you out?"

"Just your number?" There it is, the question I have been anticipating all night from this man. When you work in a bar as long as I have, you can get a good feel on men. The ones who are here to drink, those who are waiting for their buddies, the ones who are looking for a fight. They all have a look about them.

From the moment this guy sat down I could tell he was looking for a piece of ass, and us bartenders have a reputation for sleeping around. In my younger days, I would have. But now, at my age it isn't worth the hassle.

I send him a small smile and shake my head.

"No?" He presses his hand to his heart, feigning hurt at my response to his request.

"No," I return sweetly, not wanting to hurt my tip. But needing to be clear.

"Then your name at least." He holds out his hand for mine. I look down at it, not moving.

"Emily," I say and turn back to cleaning the bar.

"Emily," he rolls my name around on his tongue as if he is sampling a wine and testing it out for fullness and body.

"Mmmhmm," I tell him absentmindedly as I set his bill on the bar next to his hand.

He tosses some cash down on top of the receipt and stands.

"See you around, Em," he tells me and disappears through the bar.

She hardly looked at me the entire night. Pretending I was just another patron at her filthy bar. Flirting with other men right in front of me. Disgraceful. I won't have it. I simply won't.

Theo

Sitting in my car in the parking lot, I watch as Emily emerges from the side door of the building, the other bartender and a few busboys I watched throughout the night are by her side.

When she puts her car in reverse and backs out of the space it occupies, I put mine in drive and follow her out onto the road. I need to know she makes it home safely. Need to protect her, even if she won't let me claim her as my mate.

When we reach the house and Emily pulls into the driveway I continue to drive on by. I can't let her see me. Can't let her know I followed her here and am now following her around like a lost dog. I can't help myself. My wolf wants her, needs to claim her, to protect her.

I park down the street and get out of my car, watching as she crosses the driveway and tosses what looks like a bouquet of flowers in the trashcan sitting next to the house. Once she is safely inside the house I get back in my car and head for my hotel.

I need to call Alaric. I need to see what advice Sasha and he have for me with her sister. I need to get my head on straight and get a plan to bring her back home with me. She may be blocking out the memories of us together, but I cannot, I refuse to let go of them.

The phone rings in my ear as I head down the road in the night, I slam on the breaks as I see something large, and black cross the road in front of me.

"Shit!"

"You all right?" Alaric asks, the call having connected.

"Yea, I'm fine. Just almost hit something in the road. I swear it looked like a wolf." I shake my head to clear my mind and go back to my call.

"What's up, bro?" Alaric asks.

"Nothing much. How are Sasha and the baby doing?" I've only been gone a day and it hurts to be away from them. Away from my family.

Sasha, Alaric's wife, and I have a bond that cannot be described, and I feel it with their daughter too. I want to be back home with them. Back with my pack.

"They're good. Just sleeping a lot. Have you seen Emily? Talked to her yet? Told her you followed her home like a lost puppy?" Alaric teases.

"Shut up," I scoff into the phone.

"So why did you call?" Alaric is clearly irritated with my response.

"I don't know." I sigh. "Why does this have to be so hard?" I go on.

"Like it was just rainbows and sunshine for Sash and me?" he asks.

"No. I didn't mean that." I turn into the parking lot of the motel as I tell him this.

"I know you didn't. But they're hardheaded women. Not the easiest to love." I can hear him shrug through the phone, the sound of his clothes rustling as he paces.

"No shit," I tell him, putting the car in park and sitting in the silence for a long while. "Ask Sasha what her advice is for me, will you?"

"Will do," he tells me.

"All right, brother. I'll talk to you tomorrow."

"Night." He ends the call and I head for my lonely motel room. Another night without Emily in my arms. Another night wishing, I had the answers for how to remedy that.

Emily

When I pull into the driveway, I look down at my purse sitting on top of the crushed flowers that I had forgotten about. Having crushed them on my way out of the house and then again when I slammed my purse on top of them in my rush to get home at the end of my shift.

I pick them up now and examine them. No card, no note, no sign of who they're from. I assume they were delivered to the wrong house and feel bad for whoever didn't get them. The poor woman they were meant for waiting for a sign from her lover.

Shrugging, I take them with me and head to the trashcan, opening the lid and tossing them inside.

I scan the wood line behind the house when I see something large move in the shadows. I think I catch a glimpse of it for just a moment, a wolf.

"That isn't possible," I tell myself, trying to ease my own nerves.

I close the lid to the trashcan and look back up. There is nothing there. I don't see any signs of movement in the darkness behind the house.

"It's just your imagination, Em. You're seeing him everywhere." I tell myself again. I thought for a minute this evening that I saw Theo crossing through the crowd of people at the bar, when I looked again it was just another stranger, another face in the crowd.

As soon as I am in the house, I lock the door behind me and flip the switch to turn on the lights. It feels good to be home. To be back in my space. I miss Sasha, but before she left to go back to Alaric, she had been gone, away at school, for six years. I am used to living without her here with me. I consider calling her, but with the current time and the fact that she has a newborn, I don't want to bother my sister. She deserves to get some sleep. She has been through a lot this past year and if it were me, I would want to sleep away the memories.

Setting my purse on the table next to the front door, I head for the kitchen. As I make myself a sandwich and think about my plans for the next day, I stand in front of the calendar on the wall, then pull a slip of paper from my pocket and copy dates onto the calendar from it. Studying my schedule, I realize, I'm not going to have much time to get back into the swing of things. I have to work almost every night this week. But it will help to make up for the month of pay and tips I lost while I stayed with Sasha in the mountains, waiting for Alexandria to be born.

Finishing off my sandwich, I rinse my plate, and put it in the dishwasher. Heading for the shower I pause, halfway down the hall. A noise in the back bedroom startles me and I squint into the darkness. I know it can't be Binx, he is still with my friend, Clara, who volunteered to cat sit while I was away. I don't like having the old house empty, without my trusted friend any sound seems suspicious to me. When he is here, I can write off the strange creeks and groans in the night as my silly old cat.

I shrug when I don't hear another sound, or see anything down the hall. Heading to the bathroom I quickly undress and turn on the hot water. Waiting for it to get warm I examine myself in the mirror. I haven't showered in two days and wish I had had time to before my shift. Now, my feet ache and I simply want to curl in my bed and go to sleep. But the long drive yesterday and my long shift have me feeling grimy and I know that a shower will help lift my mood.

I think about Theo again as I stand under the scalding water and wash away two days' worth of grime and regrets. I think about the look on his face when I told him I was leaving after Sasha had the baby and that I wouldn't stay with him. Wouldn't give us a chance. He can simply be my brother-in-law, whom I see on holidays and at family gatherings. There is no need to make it more complicated than that. No need to bring emotion into it. My emotions for that man are confusing at best. Detrimental to my health at worst. I couldn't possibly fall in love with him, with a werewolf. That is madness. Look at where it got Sasha.

They're not safe, the lot of them. Trouble follows them and I don't need to be roped into it. Still, when I close my eyes, I see his looking back at me. The water cascades down over my body and I imagine it is his hands on me again. I push my back to the cool tile wall and toss my head back, the heat of the water on my front and the cold sensation of the tile on my back just as confusing a mix of feelings as my emotions are for Theo in this moment.

"Shit." I stamp my foot, turn off the tap, and climb from the shower.

Given time this will fade. My life will go back to normal. Things will most certainly be better in the morning after a good night's sleep in my own bed. Tomorrow I will see Clara, get Binx back here with me and go back to leading my mundane life, just like I always have.

Chapter 4

I STAND OUTSIDE *her bedroom window, watching as Emily comes into the room. Towel wrapped around her body. Her wet hair falling down in loose curls around her shoulders. I imagine what it would be like to hold her in this moment. To take her in my arms and kiss her. I suck in a sharp breath as she drops the towel from around her body. She is gorgeous. Her wet skin glistens in the pale light from the lamp on her nightstand.*

She crosses to the dresser, opening the top drawer and pulling out a small pink vibrator. The sound of it buzzing floats to me through the pane of glass. I watch as she spreads out on her bed, knees bent, letting them fall to the sides and exposing her pussy for me to view perfectly through the window from my position. Imagining what it would be like to be buried inside her as she calls my name, I watch as she slides a hand down over her body. Pleasuring herself.

Is she thinking of me, I wonder? Does she pull my face into her mind as she slips her fingers in and out of her slick heat?

Slipping my hand inside the front of my pants I find myself hard and ready. I jerk myself as I watch her through the window. My breath fogging the glass. When she cries out it is the sweetest sound I have ever heard, and I reach my own climax. Swallowing my own moans hard, they get caught in my throat. I freeze when she looks up toward the window.

Emily

I have an image of Theo in my mind as I continue to slide my fingers over my clit. I come, hard, imagining him buried deep inside me. When I hear what sounds like a muffled moan, I freeze. Eyes flying to the window. All I can see is the reflection of my own room staring back at me. I rise from the bed and cross to it. Pulling the curtains closed and turning around. Unable to shake the uneasy feeling of being watched, I look back over my shoulder at the now closed curtains.

Clearing my mind of the thoughts, I bend and pick up my discarded towel from the floor and hang it over the edge of the hamper next to my dresser. When I curl in bed and close my eyes, the darkness settling around me I see his face again. Theo, lying in his bed, holding me after we made love.

"Stay with me, Emily? Don't go back." He poured his heart out to me in that moment. In those words, and I crushed him.

"No. I have to. I can't stay here. This isn't my life. It may be the life Sasha has chosen to live, but I will not do the same. I need my reality." The idea of werewolves and vampires is still so foreign to me. Now, thinking back, it is so strange in that moment to think that I had been with one of them. That he'd held me in his arms.

By the time I woke the next morning Theo was gone. No longer sleeping in bed next to me. I returned to my own room that night and each night after. Our long nights awake by the fire on the patio out back spent talking about our lives and our dreams for the future were a thing of the past. I had shattered the illusion that night. Shattered Theo's heart with it, and I could tell from the look in his eyes every time he looked in my direction afterward that he couldn't stand the sight of me. I roll over in my bed, unable to get the image of his face out of my mind. Unable to sleep. Finally, it falls over me, the cloak of exhaustion. But when it does, I dream of him, of his smile, his laugh, his kiss.

Theo

I watch the next morning as Emily crosses the sidewalk to her car. Today is not the day. She has a stern look on her face, her mouth is set, and she is determined. Determined to do what, I do not know, but if I approached her now things would not go my way. Of that, I am sure.

I don't follow her as she backs out of the driveway and heads down the road. Instead, I sit and imagine being on the couch with her in her living room again. The day we first met. Long after Sasha went to sleep, we stayed awake talking, like old friends. I imagine being inside that house again, with her in my arms this time. Smiling up at me as she laughs about her childhood memories.

Pictures of them cover the walls, images of her and her family. Images of her at all different ages, with her parents, with Sasha. I smile at the memory of them. Happy that she has them and that she was willing to share them with me. Sad that I will not get to share in them again. Not now, not yet at least. Pulling away from the curb I glance in my mirror one last time at the house and think that tomorrow will be a better day.

Emily

I stop to get a coffee and as I sit in the drive thru I look up across the empty field in front of me. I see it then, a wolf standing in the edge of the trees. When I blink it is gone. He is gone. There for a split second and then gone the next. I have to stop imagining him everywhere I go. Theo is not here, he doesn't care for me any longer.

I hurt him the night I told him I wouldn't stay. Broke his heart and he never looked at me the same, he wouldn't waste his time on me now. Wouldn't follow me over five hundred miles across the country and beg me to come back to him.

"Ma'am?" The barista at the drive thru gets my attention and hands me my drink. I nod and smile at her as I look up again at the empty field and the trees standing along the edge of it. There is nothing there, no signs of him, no signs of it being real.

When I reach Clara's house it is nearly noon. I have to pick up Binx and get him home, then head to the grocery store and still get ready for tonight's shift at the bar.

"Hey, you're later than you said you would be," Clara greets me when she opens the front door.

"I know. I overslept. I had a hard time falling asleep last night after I got off work. How is my baby?" I ask her as I step into her living room and look around for Binx.

"Hey Binxy!" I call to him when I see him sprawled on the back of her sofa.

"He is good. I am going to miss him, he has really grown

on me since you've been gone." Clara closes the front door behind her.

"Really?" I look over at her, shocked at her admission as I scratch behind the black cat's ears.

"No, not really. I hate cats." She laughs. "I have been taking twice my regular dose of allergy pills since you dropped him off and my eyes are still itching like crazy. I'm glad you're home and he is going back with you. It is like he knows I am allergic to him, and he won't leave me alone," she finishes.

"Aw, is that true?" I turn to the cat, and he stretches out a paw at me, meowing. "He says you're exaggerating."

"Sure he does. I'll get his carrier." Clara leaves the room and I scoop up the cat and snuggle him to my chest.

"I missed you!" I coo.

"Aw, I missed you too, Em," Clara tells me as she reenters the room.

"I was…I mean. Yes, I missed you too, Clara," I tell her, ashamed that I was gushing to my cat and ignoring my friend who did me this huge favor.

"Want to come by the bar tonight and hang out with me? Drinks on me," I tell her as I stuff Binx into his carrier.

"Well, of course then!" She beams at me.

"Great! I have to go. But I want to catch up. I need to get some errands run before work. I'll see you around nine?" I wave to her as I pause on the front porch, waiting for her confirmation of our plans.

"Of course. See you then! Goodbye, you flea bitten thing!" She waves sweetly at Binx in the carrier.

"Don't you dare. He does not have fleas!" I glare at her.

"See you later, Em!" Clara blows me a kiss and closes the front door.

With Binx settled into the back seat of the car, I head for home. About halfway there I notice a sedan behind me, following too closely. I look in the rearview mirror, tense at having someone so close behind me. As I make a turn it follows. Then again it does the same. When I turn onto my road it drives on past and doesn't follow me again. I breathe a sigh of relief. I hate when people tailgate me. It puts me on edge and I'm shaky from having him follow so close behind me.

The moment I open the front door I know something is wrong. There is broken glass on the floor that crunches beneath my feet. Gently I set the cat carrier down on the ground just inside the doorway and scan the room.

I turn to set my purse down on the table next to the door and notice the lamp is knocked over and the photo of Sasha and me from her graduation is missing. Looking around the room as I step into the house, I check for other signs someone has been here. Is here. Thinking better of it before I head down the hall, I turn, picking up the cat carrier and go back to the front porch.

I dial 911 and wait for the line to be answered.

"911, what is the location of your emergency?" the soft female voice on the other end of the line asks.

I rattle off my address and wait, listening to the clicking of keys on the other end of the phone.

"What is the nature of your emergency? Do you need medical attention?" She comes on the line again.

"Um? Oh no. Someone has broken into my home," I tell her about the broken glass by the front door and that I did notice a missing picture, but left the house before investigating further.

"Please hold on the line, and do not reenter your home. I have units en route."

"Thank you," I tell her, taking Binx back to the car and setting him in the passenger seat. I close the door, blocking out his howls at having been so close to being freed from his carrier, but now finding himself back in the car.

The police arrive shortly, and I explain to the officers what has happened. I watch as they head into the house to investigate. Two police cruisers sit in the driveway behind my car. I stand away from the house, waiting for them to emerge from the front door.

As the minutes tick by I hear a familiar voice call my name.

"Emily!" Turning, I see Theo coming up the sidewalk toward me. My heart stops. Maybe I haven't been imagining it? Maybe he has been here all along and I did see him last night and this morning in the woods? What is he doing here?

"Theo? What are you doing here?" I ask him, confusion over the afternoon's events and now Theo's arrival at my house have me on edge and I'm left unable to process what he is saying to me.

"Ma'am?" I hear an officer calling to me from the house.

"Oh, um. Theo. Give me just a minute," I interrupt him and turn to face the men now standing on the porch.

"There doesn't appear to be anyone in the home. Would you mind coming inside with us and looking around to see if you notice anything missing?" I simply nod at him and follow the officers inside.

Theo comes closely behind me.

"Ma'am? Do you know this gentleman?" one of them asks me, putting his hand out to stop Theo from entering through the front door.

"Yes. He is my brother-in-law. You can let him in." I wave my hand signaling for him to let Theo pass, still confused by his sudden appearance here.

"Are you all right?" Theo asks me.

"Yes. I turn to him. Someone broke into my house while I was out." I follow the officers through the living room, looking around for any signs of other missing belongings.

"Really?" His confusion clearly matching my own, Theo is close on my heels.

Halfway down the hall I notice an empty spot on the wall and come to a stop.

"There is another missing picture. One from my graduation." I point at the empty nail now left in the place the picture used to hang.

When we reach my bedroom the dresser drawers are open, clothes litter the floor.

"Oh my God." My hand flies to my mouth.

I feel exposed, dirty, naked, in front of these three men with all of my belongings scattered around the room.

"Is anything missing in here, ma'am?" One of the officer's has a pen and pad in his hand.

"Honestly, it is hard to say. Can I get everything cleaned up? Make a list and get back to you?" I ask him, spinning in a circle. Examining my private space that has been invaded, not only once by the intruder, but now by these men as they investigate it.

"Yes, of course. We find that sometimes with break-ins people will find things missing in the coming days or weeks. As they go to use something they will notice it is gone." Nodding at his words I look around the room again. Toeing the pile of dirty laundry turned out of my hamper.

"Who would do this?" Theo asks, clearing his throat when all eyes turn to him.

"Well, it is a safe neighborhood, Sir. But vandals often break-in looking for valuables. Have you been away, on a trip recently, left the house unattended? I saw the cat in the carrier. Are you just returning home?" the officer continued.

"Yes, I was away for about a month, visiting my sister," I tell him, still trying to process everything.

"Then more than likely they had noticed the home empty and were looking for anything they could steal and sell. Something must have spooked them, as the big-ticket items are still here. The only things you noticed missing were the two photos?" He makes notes on his notepad as he speaks.

"Yes, everything else seems to be here," I confirm.

"Ma'am, have you noticed anyone hanging around more often than usual? Someone at your workplace maybe?" The other officer steps forward as he asks the question.

"No. Not that I can say. I mean, I have my regulars. Some of them get a little too friendly at times. But no one sending off any red flags. The occasional random guy will ask for my number. But again, nothing out of the ordinary there." I try not to sound too conceited when I say this. "Why?" I'm not sure where he is going with this line of questions.

"Often times when we see these kinds of things taken, photos, or mementos it is... Well, there is no easy way to say this. It is something we see in a lot of stalking cases." The officer shrugs at me.

"You think someone is stalking Emily?" Theo bursts out.

"I'm saying we often see it in cases like that, not in your more traditional break-ins. Let me leave you my card. If you notice anything else that is missing, please make a list and give me a call." I nod as he hands me his card.

"You two have a look around. Take your time and if you need us, we are only a call away." I nod again, as the second officer speaks.

"Thank you." Theo puts his hand out to him, shaking it and walking them toward the front door.

I stay behind, in my disheveled bedroom, trying to decide where to start cleaning up.

"Well, I guess I'm not getting my errands run before work," I tell Theo when he comes back in the house. "I need to get Binx out of the car and get the glass by the front door cleaned up. Shit! How am I going to cover that window, so the cat doesn't get out?" Realizing now that the broken window framing the front door will be an issue with Binx.

"Leave that to me. I can handle that while you go to work if you need me to, Em." I turn and look at him again when he tells me this.

"What are you doing here?" I ask him again. Not having heard the response he gave me when we were in the driveway.

"I came to see you. I needed to check up on you. I'm glad I came when I did." I nod at his words, still dazed.

"Yea, well, if you don't mind helping with the window. I really do need to get this cleaned up and get ready for work." I smile at him.

"Of course. Go get the cat out of the car and I will get started on cleaning up the glass. Do you have a trash bag and some duct tape? I can tape it up temporarily while I run to the hardware store and grab some boards."

"Yep, under the kitchen sink." I point as we head down the hall and I make my way out to get Binx from the car.

The police cruisers are gone by the time I reach the driveway. Getting the yowling cat out of the car, I take him into the house.

"I'm just going to lock him in the back bedroom," I call to Theo, who I can hear rummaging around under my kitchen sink.

I drop Binx off in the room, closing the door tightly behind me, so he cannot get out, and head back to my bedroom. I start by scooping up the dirty laundry on the floor and shoving it back into the overturned hamper as I set it upright. Looking around at the clothes scattered on the floor I sigh. It is going to take me hours to fold and put all of them away. Picking up a handful of underwear I shove them in my top dresser drawer. I stop a moment and look down. The drawer is completely empty. All of my underwear and bras are on the floor in front of the dresser. I look around, pushing them aside with my foot.

"Where is it?" I ask, continuing to search.

"Where is what?" I jump at Theo's question.

When I turn Theo is standing in the doorway, arms crossed over his chest. His biceps straining against the sleeves of his t-shirt.

"Well…" I hesitate a moment, "my vibrator is missing."

Theo looks at me, his eyebrows raised. "I'll get a notepad and you can make a list." I notice the blush on his cheeks and smile.

"Top drawer next to the trashcan in the kitchen." I give him directions to the junk drawer on his way out of the room.

"Emily!" I hear Theo calling me from the kitchen, look around the room and decide it is a lost cause for the afternoon, since I have to be at work in a couple of hours anyway.

"What is it?" I call to him as I make my way down the hall.

"Didn't you throw this away last night?" Theo is pointing at a bouquet of flowers sitting in a vase on the kitchen table. I freeze at his words and the vase. Not sure which has me more on edge, the fact that they are back here in my kitchen, or that he knows that I threw them out last night. It must have been him in the woods behind the house last night. It had to have been him this morning in the field by the coffee shop. I'm certain of it now.

"How did you—" I look at him and the sheepish look on his face makes me pause.

"I got in yesterday. I was at the bar last night. I followed you home, but didn't know what to say." He shrugs. It was him in the crowd last night. An uneasy feeling comes over me, but the look on his face tells me he meant no harm by it.

"Theo—" I pinch the bridge of my nose, sighing. "Theo," I start again, "I told you. This isn't going to work between us. I really just… it was a mistake. What happened back at the cabin. I shouldn't have led you on."

"Emily—" he starts, but I hold my hand up to stop him.

"I appreciate your offer to help with the window. I really do. But I need to get things cleaned up and get ready for work, or I'm going to be late. I'm sure it will be fine for the night. I'll have someone come out and take care of it tomorrow." I take a step towards the vase on the table.

"I'm not leaving you in a house where anyone can just walk in during the night, Emily. I'll fix the window while you're at work. I hear what you're saying. I won't bring it up again." I nod at his words.

"Thank you, Theo." Picking up the vase of flowers on the table I turn to the trash can and dump them inside. Slamming the lid on top of them.

"You did throw those away last night, though. Didn't you?" he asks. Realizing now that he may have been the one to leave them, I turn to him quizzically.

"I did. They were on the porch when I left for work yesterday. It is the strangest thing." I shrug. "Did you leave them for me?"

Theo shakes his head. It is strange, the flowers, them being here yesterday and now back in the house today. But if he says he didn't leave them, I trust him. I don't for a second think Theo would have been the one to break into my home, only to show up moments after the police under the guise of checking in on me.

Heading to my bedroom, I quickly grab something to wear that isn't in a pile on the floor and get dressed. Then I sit down in the middle of the floor and start folding clothes. I do this for what seems like hours. As the time ticks away, I think about the events of the past two days. The wolf I kept seeing. The break-in. Theo being here now. It is all too much to handle, I stand from the pile of clothes, looking down at the dent I have made in them. I can't stand to be here any longer, in this room. In the house with Theo. I decide to head to work.

"Here." I hand Theo a key when I come back to the living room, he is measuring out the window with a measuring tape, writing down the measurements on the pad of paper he got from the drawer in the kitchen.

"What is it?" he asks as I drop the keychain into his hand.

"My spare key. Lock up when you're done?" I ask. "I need to head to work."

"I'll wait for you to get home and make sure you're safe inside before I go," he tells me, trying to hand me the key back.

I know not to fight him on this. I know he isn't going to leave now no matter how hard I try. I can see it in the look in his eyes. "No, you need it. You'll need to lock the door when you head to the hardware store, you'll need the key to get back in when you get back," I insist.

"If, you're sure." He shrugs. "But I am still going to wait for you to get home."

I nod. "Thank you," I tell him. "Oh, can you make sure you let Binx out when you're done with the window? He shouldn't be locked up all night."

"Sure thing, Em. I'll see you later."

"See you later." I wave as I head for the front door.

Chapter 5

I WATCH HER GO, *leaving the house behind as she gets into her car and pulls out of the driveway. I reach in my pocket and wrap my hand around the crumpled pair of her underwear I have stashed there. A piece of her in my fist. Licking my lips, I smile. We will be in for a fun night tonight, my Emily and me. I wait until she is gone, then turn back toward the house. There is only one problem. One thing standing in the way, and I will be sure to eliminate that as soon as possible.*

Emily

Clara shows up right on time. I'm relieved to see her and clear a spot on the bar for her as she approaches.

"Hey!" she chirps at me. "Oh no, that rough of a night already?"

"Sit down, you have no idea," I tell her. "The regular?" Pulling a glass from under the counter I watch as she nods. I fix her drink and turn around to set it on the bar in front of her.

When I do I notice the same man from last night now sitting at the bar next to my friend.

"Hey stranger," I greet him. "Whiskey sour?" I ask. Pulling another glass from under the counter.

"Hey, beautiful girl. Whiskey sour." He smiles at me. I get the same strange feeling I did last night as he looks me over. The hairs on the back of my neck are on end again.

After I set his drink down in front of him, I turn my attention back to Clara.

"So, what's up buttercup?" she asks me, sipping her drink.

"Someone broke into my house. While I was at your place this afternoon." Clara gasps at my words. I notice the man on the stool next to her look in our direction. He is listening. They always are, his type.

"I know, right! I had to call the cops and everything." I shrug at her. Not wanting to make a big deal of it or give out too much information when I know this conversation is not our own.

"Do you want to come stay with me tonight?" she offers. I think it through. Wonder if I should call Theo and tell him to go home. Tell him I am going to stay with Clara and that he doesn't need to worry about me. But the pull to see him again is strong and I decide against going to Clara's.

"No. I think it's fine. No big deal. The cops say it may be because I was on my trip for so long and someone noticed the house was empty, so broke in looking for stuff to sell." I shrug. I don't tell her the truth. I don't want her to worry, or to push me further on this right now. Not when we are being so closely listened to.

Theo will be there when I get home. I'm not ready to have to explain that to her, who he is and what happened between us, it is all too messy. I don't want to go down that road yet. Not when I'm still so shaken from his showing up this afternoon.

Clara and I make small talk, she catches me up on the happenings around town while I was away for a month. Gives me the cliff notes version of her dating life from that time.

"Oh, that reminds me!" Clara sets her glass down. "I forgot to tell you. I met the perfect guy for you."

"Clara," I say and roll my eyes at her. Then glance at Mr. Whiskey Sour. He is listening again. Ears perked when she says this.

"No! Vince is perfect! He started working with me about three weeks ago and you two would really hit it off. Let me set you up with him, please!" she whines.

"Fine," I agree at last. "Fine. Set it up," I sigh.

"Perfect!" She pulls her phone from her purse. "I'll send him your number right now. But then I have to go. It is getting late, and I have a date."

"You just said it was getting late, how can you have a date?" I ask Clara.

She wiggles her eyebrows at me. Getting her meaning, I shake my head.

"Do you need a refill?" I turn to the man sitting next to her. Who has been so obviously eavesdropping on our conversation the entire night.

"Sure," he says. Clearly not a man of many words tonight, it is possible his ego is still bruised from my turning him down when he asked for my number before.

I pour him another drink then lean across the bar and kiss Clara on the cheek.

"See you!" she calls to me as she hops down from her stool and heads across the bar.

"I couldn't help but overhear," says the man now sitting

on the stool that Clara just left, scooting closer to me in the corner of the bar.

"Yea?" I ask. Pissed that he is acting like it wasn't blatantly obvious he was listening in.

"Someone broke into your house?" he asks me.

"Yes, but they didn't really take anything," I shrug, "so, it's fine." I don't offer more and make to turn to tend to my other customers. When he starts to speak again, I stop and face him.

"I'm sorry to hear about that. Do you want a ride home tonight? Maybe your friend is right, and you should go stay with her? Wouldn't you feel safer?" His words carry a warning to me and something inside me screams that if I were ever to get into a car with this man I wouldn't see the light of day again.

"No, thanks. I'm fine. Really," I tell him, trying to shrug him off.

I go back to clearing the bar and getting ready to shut down for the night.

"Well then, how about your number?" He smiles at me again.

"Look, I told you last night. No. I'm not interested," I snap at him.

"Oh, but you're willing to go out with this Vince guy your friend turned up?" I spin on him then. I'm seeing red, pissed at the audacity he is speaking to me with. Making it clear now that he was listening to our entire conversation.

"Listen, jackass! I just had some sicko break into my house, leave me flowers and steal my fucking vibrator. I told you last night, no! I have too much on my mind right now to put up with your shit. Here," I slam his bill down on the bar top. "We're closed. Pay your tab and head out, buddy." He goes silent then, tossing a handful of bills down on the counter and getting up. He turns back and looks at me.

"Goodnight, Emily," he says as he leaves the bar. A chill rolls up my spine as I watch him go.

———

Theo

I finish boarding up the window next to Emily's front door and go to let her cat out of the back room she has him locked in. He has been crying the entire time I have been working on the window.

"Come here, Binx," I call to him as I go down the hall. "Where's your bowl, buddy? You want something to eat?"

I rummage through Emily's cabinets and find a can of cat food, putting a bowl down for him on the floor I fill it. Then turn and pull a chair out at the kitchen table. Sitting down I lean back and watch the cat. Once he is done, I get the bowl cleaned up and put in the dishwasher and move to the couch. Watching TV, I drift off to sleep after a while. The sound of the long-forgotten TV show humming in the background as I doze off.

"Theo?" Emily calls my name, rousing me. "Hey Theo, I'm home." I smile at her words.

Still in my half-asleep haze I smile at the idea of Emily coming home to me after a day at work. I peek open an eye, swiping at her, grabbing around her waist and pulling her down onto the couch with me.

She giggles, and I get lost in the sound of it.

"Hey, baby." I kiss her on the cheek.

"Hey." She smiles at me. "Thank you for staying. It feels better to have you here," Emily admits to me.

I nod. "I can stay," I offer, "sleep on the couch."

I watch as she thinks it through, then shrugs. "Maybe? I mean if you want to." She is leaving it up to me and I smile.

"Want to watch TV with me?" I ask her.

"I believe you were sleeping," she points out.

"I was," I confess to her. "Let me grab my bag from the truck." Stretching as I rise from the couch, I eye Emily. Her feet curled under her, she smiles up at me and it warms my heart.

Outside of the house I catch a glimpse of movement in the bushes, leaning over the rail of the front porch I examine them closely. I don't see anything there. Hurrying to the truck, I grab my bag, and head back for the house. This time I get a good look at him as he disappears into the wood line behind the house. A dark colored wolf.

My eyebrows climb my forehead. A wolf? Here? I shake my head and walk across the yard. It must just have been a dog. Dismissing the beast, I head back toward Emily's front door. Sitting on the front porch is an envelope that I am sure wasn't there when I left to go to the truck. Turning it over in my hand when I pick it up, I see her name scrawled across the front of it.

Slipping the napkin with the bar's logo on it from the envelope I read the note scrawled on it.

Emily,

I really thought you were different. Thought we could have something together. I see the bitch you are now. Just like the rest of them. You'll regret this.

Shoving the note back in the envelope I slip it into my back pocket. I make a note to take it with me to the police department tomorrow with the list of missing things that Emily is putting together for them.

When I enter the house, I see Emily curled on the couch sound asleep. I smile down at her as I lift her in my arms and carry her to her bedroom.

"Theo," she calls to me after I lay her down and turn to leave the room. "Stay with me?" Her voice is small. I can't deny her this. I can't deny myself. I turn and head back to the bed.

Pulling my shirt off over my head, I toss it to the floor, and then slip out of my pants. When I pull the covers over top of me, Emily rolls into my body. I close my arms around her. Taking in a deep breath, I breathe in her scent.

Chapter 6

EMILY

I wake to the sounds and smells of breakfast being cooked in my kitchen. When I roll over the empty spot next to me once occupied by Theo is rumpled and it makes me smile. He spent the night with me in bed. Holding me as I slept. When I woke to a strange sound in the night, I curled into him and let him comfort me. I needed him here. I don't think I would have gotten any sleep if I was alone. I stretch out on my bed, sighing.

"Hey, sleepyhead. Breakfast is ready." When I turn, Theo is standing in the doorway, shirtless in a pair of basketball shorts and nothing else. I wonder for the first time, if maybe I was wrong. If maybe this man can fit into my life. If perhaps, we do fit together, like pieces of a puzzle.

The look of him makes it hard to breathe and I want nothing more than to call him to me in this moment. Invite him into my bed and let him make love to me again, the memories of our night together filling my mind.

"Don't look at me that way, Em," he scolds me, turning from me in the doorway and heading down the hall. I watch him go, sad both at my decision to reject him before, and his rejection of me now.

When I climb out of bed and head to the kitchen. I pass by the pile of dirty laundry overflowing from my hamper and make a mental note to start a load in the washer after I eat.

"What's for breakfast?" I ask, plopping down in a chair at the kitchen table.

The aroma of bacon grease fills the air and my stomach growls.

"Pancakes, eggs, and bacon." Theo sets a plate piled high with goodness in front of me on the table. "I'm going to go back today. Unless you want me to stay?" he asks, the light in his eyes stirs something in my heart.

I do want him to stay. It would be easier to not have to be alone with everything going on. But I know I cannot lead him on again.

"No, I think it is best if you go home, Theo," I tell him, picking up a piece of bacon and biting into it. Watching as he nods sadly.

"I'll go get dressed and get ready to head out." He turns to leave the kitchen.

I want to stop him. To tell him he doesn't have to leave right this second. To invite him to eat with me. To delay the inevitable. But I cannot, it would only make things more difficult when he does have to go.

"I'll see you around?" he asks, coming back into the kitchen. Fully dressed now, a duffle bag slung over his shoulder. The hurt in his eyes tells me everything I need to know.

I sigh. "Theo." Standing from the table I turn to face him.

"It is okay, Em. It really is." I nod, at his kindness in this moment. At his letting me off the hook for confusing him yet again with my request that he stay, not only here with me but in my bed last night.

"Goodbye." The word sounds hollow as I say it. Sounds final and I don't like it.

"Goodbye, Em. I'm just a phone call away if you need anything." He turns to leave. Then pauses with his hand on the front door.

I watch his shoulders heave with his sigh as he hesitates a moment longer. Lifting my hand, I make to say something, anything to stop him. But Theo turns the knob and disappears into the morning light, the door closing behind him. Falling into the chair at the table I sob. Head in my hands I let my tears fall unchecked.

I watch her through the back door, tears falling down her cheeks. The pain in her eyes breaking my heart. I didn't get the chance last night to tell her how I feel. To tell her it is me she is meant to be with.

Tonight, I think. Tonight, will be the night that she and I get to be together at last. I continue to watch Emily through the windows throughout the morning. Angry that I have been reduced to skulking around her home in the shadows. Keeping my distance, when I was so close before.

The smell of her on the sheets fills my memories. I bunch her panties in my fist again as I watch her go about her chores. Doing laundry and cleaning up the remainder of her bedroom. When I pull them from my pocket, I bury my nose in them and I am taken back to the moment I lay in her bed.

The moment I breathed her in and filled my mind with images of us together. "Soon," I promise her through the pane of glass. "Soon."

Theo

The drive back to the motel is silent. I don't turn on the radio. I simply roll down the windows and listen to the birds and sounds of the world around me. I contemplate turning around and going back.

Taking her in my arms and shaking some sense into her. I know she doesn't want this. Doesn't want me to go. I could see it in her face, both last night when she asked me to stay and this morning when she told me to leave. She is confused, torn, and I will win out over all else. I will convince her in the end.

But the break-in, the note in my pocket, the idea that someone out there is wanting to cause her harm stops me from actually leaving. I will return to the motel, but I will remain in town. I'll give her the time and space she needs, but I can't leave her now. Can't leave her when it is not safe, and she needs me to protect her.

Emily

"Where are they?" I ask the cat as he sits on top of the dryer while I fold the clothes, I pull from inside it.

My favorite pair of green underwear are missing. The cheekies I wore to work two nights ago. The pair I had on the night that Theo and me were together back at his cabin. They were in the hamper. I know they were. But they're not here now. I peek into the gap next to the washer, making sure they didn't fall down into it, between it and the wall while I loaded the clothes in to be washed. Nothing but some dust bunnies look up at me from the dark space.

"Strange," I tell Binx, scratching behind his ears.

I hear my phone ringing from my bedroom and leave carrying my pile of now clean laundry with me as I rush through the house.

The number on the screen is one I don't recognize.

"Hello?" I ask, connecting the call.

There is no voice on the other end of the phone, silence greets me. I pause, listening, waiting. I hear it then, deep breathing. When the phone beeps signaling that the call was ended, I see a message pop up on the screen.

"*Tonight.*"

Is all it says. My phone rings again as I hold it in my hand, and I jump.

"Hello?" I answer it again, frustration in my voice apparent.

"Emily?" A man's voice comes through the line.

"Yes?" I ask, still shaken by the previous call and subsequent message.

"This is Vince. I got your number from Clara."

"Oh," I let my voice float through the phone to him. "Did you… did you just call me?"

"Well, I called you now," he tells me, the confusion in his voice at my question is clear.

"So, I was wondering. Well, Clara had said. I guess we are being set up?" Vince stumbles over his words.

"I believe we are," I tell him.

"Are you free tonight?" I hesitate a moment. I am scheduled to work. But really could use a night off. So I think it through and plan on seeing if I can get my shift covered.

"I might be. I have to work, but let me make some calls and see if I can get my shift covered. What were you thinking?"

"Dinner?" he asks me, clearing his throat.

"Sure. Can I text you in a bit and let you know if I was able to get my schedule cleared?"

"Of course. I look forward to meeting you. I'll talk to you in a bit."

Vince ends the call and I quickly send some texts trying to get my shift covered. I'm still trying to make sense of the strange phone call before when I get a message that Katie is going to cover for me, and I won't have to work tonight. I quickly type a message to Vince and make plans to meet him at Sweetwater at eight.

That will give me time today to get my errands, I didn't get run yesterday, done and to stop by the police department to drop off the list of the few things I did find missing. Pulling a notepad from the drawer in the kitchen I see the first page covered in Theo's handwriting. His measurements for the window. Trailing my fingers over the words I feel my heart flip in my chest. Then roll my eyes at myself and the fact that something so small from this man can make me feel this way.

Flipping the page, I make my list.

1. Underwear
2. Vibrator
3. Two framed photos
4. Hairbrush

I make a small note at the bottom of the page reminding myself to mention the flowers that showed up on the kitchen table after I had gotten rid of them the night before. That being the strangest thing about the break-in.

I head to the bathroom and shower, getting myself ready to run my errands and stop by the police station before I am due to meet Vince. Once I get out of the hot shower I stand, frozen, staring at the mirror. In the fog from the heat of the steam there is a small heart in the bottom corner of the mirror. I continue to stand and stare at it, shock filling me at the thought that the person who was in my house did this. Had time to do this. I shake my head, not wanting to look at it any longer I quickly brush my hand over the mirror, clearing away the outline and denying what it means.

As I rush out of the house and turn to lock the door behind me, I notice the envelope taped to the front door. Pulling it free I open it up and slip the photo inside out of it. I drop it to the ground, stepping backward and bumping into the porch rail as I do. The image of me sleeping in my bed floats to the ground at my feet. My hand flies to my mouth and I feel like I might be sick. I squeeze my eyes closed and find the strength to pick the thing back up. When I do, I turn it over in my hand. The word written on the back sends a chill through me.

"Tonight."

It is the same word in the text message I received earlier, I had forgotten about it when Vince called and distracted me. Forgotten about it when I was greeted with the heart on my mirror as I stepped out of the shower. I need to remember these things. Need to tell the police everything that has happened, the phone call, the text, the heart on the mirror, this picture. I make a mental list as I stuff the image in my purse. Planning to take it with me to the police department.

The drive to the department is silent. I think through the ramifications of an image of me sleeping in my bed. The only person who has been in the house with me is Theo, could he be the one behind this? Why would he do such a thing? Even if he took a photo of me, the question is why leave it for me here?

As I make my way through town I look up, glancing in

my rearview mirror. Swearing that the sedan that is two cars back is the same one I noticed following too closely the other day. I chew on my lip and wonder if I should mention this to the police as well.

I drop everything off at the front desk with the stuffy receptionist who tells me that the investigator whom I spoke to previously is out of the office today. I explain the photo and the list of missing belongings to her, while she takes notes about the image, the heart on the mirror, the car following me. She assures me she will pass everything on to him and then he will be in touch with me.

Nodding, I leave the station. When I get back to my car I freeze, hand on the door handle. The feeling of being watched again is one I cannot shake. I look around behind me, scanning the parking lot and wood line. I think I see a familiar truck parked in the back corner.

"Theo?" I squint, checking the license plate I see it is an Ohio tag and couldn't be Theo's truck. I dismiss it as just being on edge and climb behind the wheel of my car. When I glance back up at the truck in my mirror before I pull out of the parking space I see him then, standing in the shadows of the trees. A wolf. Dark colored with eyes gleaming at me. Quickly I turn, and look over my shoulder through the rear window, he is gone. A figment of my imagination again? Or is Theo here, watching me, following me? I don't know what to do. I try to put it out of my mind.

When I get to the grocery store it is nearly deserted. I like shopping during the week for this reason and I speed up and down the aisles quickly getting the things I need. I'm distracted by my thoughts of the sedan following me, of the wolf I keep seeing, of the truck parked at the police department. All of this swirls through my mind as I absentmindedly toss things into my cart.

"Hey beautiful girl!" I hear a voice call to me as I

examine the selection of produce, looking for fresh green beans for dinner tomorrow.

I turn and see the man from the bar standing to my right. I flinch at the sight of him, he has caught me off guard being here, and I raise an eyebrow at him.

"Whiskey sour?" I point in his direction, pretending I'm not exactly sure who he is.

"Yep, how are you? Did you sleep well after your break-in? I thought about you last night." His words ring in my ears, and I tense.

"Yes, thank you," I tell him. Turning back to the selection of produce, I dismiss him.

"Funny running into you here. I'm new in town. This is my first trip out, need to fill the fridge. You know?" He continues to try to engage me in conversation. I shrug and push my cart away from him. Realizing only after he is behind me that he doesn't have a cart, or a basket, no shopping is actually being done as he follows behind me.

"See you around." I call back over my shoulder as I quickly exit the aisle and head for the check out. Deciding I don't need to finish my trip. I'd rather just be out of the store and in the safety of my own car.

"Tonight?" he calls to me. I freeze, turning to look at him. Thinking only of the text message and the note scrawled on the back of the image of me sleeping in my bed.

I feel the blood drain from my face as I stare into this man's eyes.

"Don't you work tonight?" he asks me then. I shake my head, dismissing my gut feeling and staring him down. Without another word I turn and head for the checkout.

Chapter 7

I SIT *at the bar long after the time that Emily was due for her shift. She never showed. I'm angry. I checked the calendar on the wall in her kitchen and she was due to be here. She should be here. Where the hell is she?*

She keeps ruining all my plans. I slam my hand down on the bar and the woman standing behind it jumps, glaring at me. When I rise and head out of the bar into the night I swear under my breath. I'll never track her down now in this damned town.

Sitting outside of Emily's house a while later I see the lights are all off inside. She isn't home. I wait. Patience is important. I need to keep my cool and not fuck this up.

Finally, I see her car turn the corner, headlights follow behind her as a second car comes down the street. When it pulls into her driveway behind her, I tense. Watching closely, a man climbs from the second car and follows her into the house. She is ruining everything.

Emily

. . .

I lead Vince into the living room after our dinner date. Turning, I smile at him. I have had too much to drink tonight. Too much has happened in the past few weeks for me to be thinking straight about the man standing before me.

Dinner went well, we hit it off, and conversation between us was easy. I learned about his family, his career, his goals in life. All the first date conversation was checked off the list. When I smile at him Vince returns my smile.

"You're beautiful," he tells me, and I giggle. The wine having gone to my head. "I'm really glad Clara suggested this," he continues as he steps into the room toward me.

"Me too. Do you want a drink?" I motion for the kitchen and flip the light on as I head into the room, pulling a bottle of wine from the cabinet and pouring us two glasses.

"Thank you." Vince takes a sip as I hand it to him.

"Listen," I pause, trying to get my words right. "I'm not looking for anything serious," I tell him. But I can't help but look at his lips, his dark hair, the cut of his jaw. He reminds me of him, of Theo. I need to have his hands on me now. To block out the memories of the man I wish was standing with me here in the kitchen.

"I get that." Vince shrugs. "I'm not here to pressure you into anything."

"I appreciate that," I tell him, taking a step closer to him. Swinging my hips as I do.

"Let's just have some fun and see where it goes," Vince tells me. I smile at him.

"That sounds good," I purr the words.

Leading him to the couch, I watch as he takes a seat. I down my wine then set my glass down on the coffee table. I toss my hair over my shoulder and straddle him. Settling onto this strange man's lap and getting lost in our kiss. As I squeeze my eyes closed, I picture Theo beneath me, imagine it is his hands sliding up my back under my shirt and unhooking my bra. His mouth on my neck as I gasp for breath. His cock I grind down on beneath me.

"Emily," Vince says and breaks the spell. I open my eyes and look into his.

Confusion at how I could ever think he compares to Theo flowing through my mind. They're different. So different. I don't care. I've started this, made it this far. I lift my arms over my head and let him slip my shirt off, tossing it to the floor. My bra follows and his hands are on my breasts then.

He is rough, clumsy, and moves too quickly as he gropes me. Dropping his mouth to my nipple he takes it in his mouth and circles his tongue over it. I toss my head back and gasp at the sensation.

"Don't stop," I tell him. I squeeze my eyes closed again and throw myself back into the memories of Theo.

When Vince lifts me off his lap and settles me onto the couch I quickly slip out of my jeans and present myself to him. I need him to fill me. I need him to slide deep within me and fuck me hard and fast. Chasing the memories of my night with Theo from my mind. I bend over the back of the couch, knees pushing into the cushions as I watch him undress over my shoulder.

When he slips a condom from his pocket and slides it down over himself, I suck in a deep breath. The wine hitting me harder now, the room starts to spin a bit. I steady myself for what is coming. For what I have put in motion. He steps up and slides into me from behind. Hard, fast, he pounds into my pussy as I clamp down around him. He is like a jackrabbit, like a teenager who has no idea what he is doing with a woman. A man on a mission to find his own climax with little care for his partner.

Digging my fingers into the back of the couch I push

myself back onto him, riding this strange man, picturing another in my mind as I do. Vince rides me hard and fast, coming quickly and collapsing onto me on the sofa. I was close, so close to finding my climax in this man's arms. It was nothing compared to the night Theo held me, and it leaves me feeling cold and angry. Frustration bubbles up inside me and I roll onto my side, glaring at him.

I don't let him stay. The puppy dog eyes he gives me as I roll over on the couch tell me he would if I asked. But I need to get him out of the house. I need to be alone, shower the scent of him off me and go to bed.

"This was fun, we should do it again sometime." I give him my old response from back in the day when I needed a man to leave.

Vince nods and gathers his belongings. When I kiss him on the cheek at the front door, closing it behind him, I look down at the board nailed to the window frame next to it. My heart hurts. I think about Theo and how I sent him away. I shouldn't have.

I storm to my bedroom, angry that I didn't find what I was looking for in Vince's arms. Even more angry at the jackass who stole my vibrator so I can't use it to get myself off now that Vince is gone. I scroll through my phone, searching for my favorite porn that I know will do the trick quickly.

As I press play, I toss myself back onto my bed, still undressed, and I slide my hand down between my legs. When I close my eyes, laying my phone down, forgotten on the bed, I listen to the sounds of the video still playing but pull the image of Theo into my mind. The night I let him make love to me back in his bed. Is a welcomed memory I sink into.

Theo slipped inside me and I wrapped my legs tightly around his waist, pulling him deeper still. I needed to feel him, needed to feel every inch of him as he made love to me.

When he dropped his head to my mouth and kissed me, our tongues intertwined in my mouth.

Taking in a deep breath I could smell him, the scent of him filling my mind and my memories.

"Open your eyes and look at me, Em." I nodded then, opening my eyes and looking deeply into his.

I lay with him the night before in his wolf form, lay with my arms wrapped around him and was unable to fathom how intimate the moment was between us. It is nothing now, compared to this. Compared to having him deep inside me and not knowing where I stop, and he begins.

Slowly he slides in and out of me again and again, for a long while. We continue our pace, staring into each other's eyes. When he slips from me I whimper, and he cups my cheek.

"It's all right, turn over." He lifts me by the hips and helps me to my hands and knees in front of him, slipping into me again. Deeper this time. Smacking my ass as he does.

I flinch at the sudden contact of his palm on my bare skin, then turn and look over my shoulder at him, smiling.

"Don't stop," I beg.

"Never," he promises in return.

I remember his hands on me, his cock inside me as I slide my fingers over my clit, lifting my other hand to my breast. Taking a nipple between my fingers and twisting it hard, the same way he did as he rode me from behind.

Vince was nothing compared to this man, this wolf, this beast.

He rode me hard and fast, then slowed his pace as he played with my breasts, as he teased my clit, all until I was panting. Begging him to let me come.

"Soon, Em. I promise." He stepped back from me again and I collapsed forward onto my stomach on the bed.

When he took hold of my ankles and pulled me to the end of the bed he immediately buried his face between my thighs. His tongue filling me where he had just been, his teeth grazing my clit.

I arched my back and let him eat me, let him devour me, body, and soul.

"I want to taste you when you come. I want to have it cover my face, running down my chin. I want to hear you scream my name as I make you come for me, Em." I nodded at his words. Letting them push me over the edge as he slipped his fingers deep inside me and stroked me gently there.

"Fuck!" I roared. "Theo! I'm going to come. Don't stop. Please don't stop." True to my word I threw myself over the edge and let the orgasm take me over, for a split second his hands left me, a split second as I began to come, he left me.

Then pounding forward into me as he filled me with his cock, the sensation pushing me over the edge again into a second orgasm. I tensed down around him and let him ride me, let him fill me as I milked him with my tight pussy.

"Oh God, Emily. I'm going to come. Don't stop yet." His hand reached down over my hip, slipping between my thighs, finding my clit again.

As he played with me, toyed with me, he marched me to the precipice again.

When I came this time, I could see stars in my vision as I squeezed my eyes closed. As I felt him swell and buck inside me. We came together. Collapsing onto the bed beside me, he took me with him, wrapped his arms around me and buried himself inside my waiting pussy again.

. . .

Opening my eyes as I call out his name, "Theo!" I reach my climax, my own fingers trailing over my body. The image of us tangled together still clear in my mind.

"Fuck," I gasp, feeling the tears pour from my eyes as I roll onto my side in my empty bed. Curling into a ball and wrapping my arms around my middle. Sobs heaving from my chest as I cry myself to sleep.

"Theo," I call to him again, more quietly this time. I need him here with me, need him to hold me now and chase away the fears from the past few days. Need to feel safe and protected in his embrace, with his kisses on my skin. Finally, I drift into a fitful sleep, dreaming of Theo, wolves, and intruders in my home. The night is relentless in it's taunting of my emotions.

I've been lying awake for hours. Thinking through the previous night and my decision, not only to go out with Vince, but to bring him back here. I roll on my side and the clock glares at me. It isn't even six I wonder if it is too early to call Theo. I grab my phone and type out the text message, reading it and rereading it again, and again. I sound desperate, pitiful even. I don't care. I take a deep breath and hit send. Setting the phone back down on the nightstand I roll onto my back and stare at the ceiling. A short while later I hear the notification tone alerting me to a new message.

I hold my breath as I reach over and read Theo's response. He is on his way. I sigh. I need to shower, I still smell like sex, and regret from last night. Jumping up, I rush to the bathroom, quickly turn on the water and step under before it has a chance to warm fully.

When I step out of the shower it is still there, the small heart in the corner of the mirror, the streaks from me swiping my hand over it break through the center of it. But it is still there taunting me. A message from the stranger who invaded my space, who violated me and my home in the process. I stop and stare.

I don't have time to dry my hair, I quickly rub it dry with a towel and apply a bit of eye makeup, then head to make coffee. The pot is still brewing when I hear the soft knock on the front door. I cross the living room and open the front door, expecting to see Theo standing on the other side. Instead, when I open the door no one is there. Sitting on the front porch mat is a bouquet of flowers, deep red roses. Just like before. Bending down I scoop them up and carry them into the house, closing the front door behind me. When I set them on the kitchen table, I notice this time there is a note.

"My dearest Emily, I have tried again and again to get you to notice me. Do not discount what we could have together. I can make you my world, my Queen, my dearest."

A chill runs up my spine I get the feeling instantly of being watched again and look around the kitchen. A knock on the door makes me nearly jump out of my skin and I rush to open it.

Theo is standing on the other side of the door this time.

"Hey," he greets me with a soft smile.

"Hey!" I return his greeting.

"What's wrong? You're white as a sheet." Theo steps into the house and reaches for me.

I take a step backward from him, leery of the man standing in front of me.

"Did you leave me flowers?" I ask him as I turn and close the door behind him when he steps into the living room.

"Flowers? No. What's going on?" Theo spots the bouquet on the kitchen table and crosses to it. "These?" he points at them. "I didn't send you these, Em." Lifting the note, he reads it carefully before he sets it back down on the kitchen table.

"I don't know what is going on, Theo. The break-in, the flowers, the photo on the front porch—"

"What photo?" he interrupts me.

I take my time and explain the photo, the phone call, and the text message I received. Theo looks at me like I have two heads.

"Emily, I'm worried you're in danger. Did you tell the police all of this?" He pauses for a moment. "I found a letter on your front porch the other night. Em, I think they might be right. I think you have a stalker."

"A letter, what letter?" I ask him, confused.

"It was written on a napkin from your work, it was, well it was rather threatening. I have it in the truck. I was going to give it to you to turn in to the police."

"Theo, I don't understand why this is happening, who would be doing this?"

"I don't know, Em. I really don't, but we will get to the bottom of it." Theo takes a step toward me and opens his arms. I fall forward into them, letting him wrap them around me and hold me tightly to his chest. "I'm not going to let anything happen to you."

I nod, letting the tears I have been holding back slip down my cheeks.

"Theo, I'm scared," I confess.

"I know. It is going to be okay. I promise you this. I'm not going to let anything happen." He tells me again. "I promise. Have you eaten? Do you want breakfast?"

Nodding, I step backward from his embrace.

Theo

. . .

I make Emily breakfast as I think through all of the information, she gave me about what has been happening. I wish she had been honest with me sooner about things. But I understand her hesitation to say anything. The truth of it all becomes more real once you speak these things out loud and it is clear that she is scared.

Once we fix breakfast we sit and eat in silence, it is deafening. Neither of us knowing what to say. Finally, I break the silence.

"Emily, would you be willing to come home with me?" I have been thinking this through. With the pack's help, even if this person was able to find us after we left, I could protect her better. I go on, telling her, "If you leave, if we leave. Then maybe this person will leave you alone, not follow you. Even if they do. I could protect you. The pack could protect you."

She looks up at me, tears filling her eyes. "How do we even know this isn't the pack doing this? That this isn't because of the pack? Look at what happened to Sasha. Trouble follows you, you're werewolves for fuck's sake, who is to say you're any safer?"

The accusation stings and I just look into her eyes. She is blaming me for this, blaming what I am, and the pack.

"Emily, I don't think this is about us. I don't see how it could be, or who would be behind it. I honestly think I could protect you. Let me help you, Emily." Reaching across the table I close my hand over hers.

"Theo? I don't know. I don't know what is happening and I don't think I can leave with you."

"Then I'm staying." I don't give her an option in this. "I'm going to stay with you until we get to the bottom of this.

If you won't leave with me then this is the only other choice, and it isn't negotiable."

"Theo…"

"Emily. I'm not going to budge on this. I'll check out of the motel today and stay here with you. End of discussion."

"You can't just barge in here like a caveman and tell me what to do!" She stands from the table, shouting at me.

"You're my mate, Emily. I am not going to leave you to fend for yourself in this. I am not going to turn my back on you and leave you unprotected!" Realizing only too late what I have said.

"Your mate?" She stares at me.

Running my hands over my face and through my hair, I sigh. I didn't intend to tell her this way.

"Your fucking mate?" She yells when I don't respond.

"Emily, please calm down—"

"So, you have some wolfy claim on me because you think I'm your mate? This is ridiculous, Theo!"

"Emily, please." I reach my hands out to her and try to pull her to me, she spins and turns out of my grasp.

"I can't believe this. I can't do this. I don't want to do this, Theo. I want to be normal. I wanted to come home to my regular everyday life and be normal. Now some sicko is stalking me, you're saying I'm your mate, and I don't know how to process any of this. This isn't fair. Don't I get a say in any of it?"

"Of course, you do! Just not in my decision to stay. I'm not leaving you with this guy out there threatening you."

Emily sighs and turns from me, leaving the room. I stand alone in the kitchen, looking around at the space trying to decide what to do next, if I should follow her, or not. Deciding, I storm after her through the house.

"Emily!" I yell her name down the hall.

"Theo, don't! Don't do this right now!" she calls to me from her bedroom.

"We are doing this right now. I'm not going to let this end right here." I enter the bedroom and her eyes are red rimmed and full of tears as she looks across the room at me.

My insides twist and I feel my heart sink. I cross to her, take her in my arms and hold her tightly to my chest. The flood gates open then, and she weeps as I hold her.

"I'm scared," she whispers softly.

"I know. So am I." The confession stings, I'm supposed to be brave enough for both of us, not scared of things that go bump in the night. "Look at me." Placing my hand under her chin I tilt her face up toward me and look into her eyes. "I promise you I will not let anything happen to you, Emily."

She nods, and I watch as her tongue passes over her lower lip just before she chews on the corner of it. The look in her eyes, the tempting glisten on her lip calls to me. I tip my head to her and close my mouth over Emily's.

"Theo," she breathes out my name.

"Mmm?" I ask as I continue to kiss her, not letting up the pressure on her mouth. I can feel her tense then, I prepare for her to push me away, to reject me in this moment. But I don't give in and that is when it happens. Her body melts into mine. Arms wrap around my neck and she pulls me down to her, I kiss her hungrily then. Like a man on a deserted island seeing water for the first time. I need this. I need her.

———

Emily

. . .

I let Theo kiss me for a moment, I consider pushing him away, turning him down, ending this here and now. But I cannot. I need to feel his kiss, to feel his hands on me. I relax into him and let him kiss me, kissing him back then.

When I step backward from him the look of fear and rejection in his eyes breaks my heart. I shake my head. Reaching down I take the hem of my shirt in my hands and pull it off over my head. I stand before him in my bra and pants, slipping my hand down to my button I undo it and slowly push the fabric of my pants down over my hips.

"Emily, you're gorgeous." Theo's words ring in my ears, and I am thrown back to the night we were together back at his cabin.

"Theo?" I take another step backward toward the bed, sitting on the edge of it. "Make love to me?" My request is quiet, as if saying it out loud makes it all too real.

"If I do this. I'm not taking it back, Emily. I am not going to play this game where you use me when you want me then toss me out on my ass the next second. If we do this, this is it between us." The finality of his words makes me pause.

Do I want this? Do I want to be with this man? I do. In my heart I know I do. But I can't turn my mind off and stop all the questions swirling there.

I nod at him.

"Say it, Emily." Theo's voice is deep and commanding.

"Theo, make love to me please. I want to do this. I want to be with you." I watch as he processes my request and then nods. Taking a step toward me.

When he lowers his body over mine on the bed he covers me with his own. His arms, pinning mine above my head as he kisses me again. I feel his leg between mine, parting them for him to settle there. The bulge in his pants pushing against the soft fabric of my underwear. I moan into his mouth as the pressure he applies to my groin grows the flame inside me. Theo walks himself down the length of my body, his hands on either side of me on the bed. When he reaches my hips he hooks his fingers under the waistband of my underwear and pulls them down gently over my thighs. Tossing them to the side.

I watch as he settles onto his knees on the floor at the edge of the bed and lowers his mouth to me. Sucking in a sharp breath when his tongue meets my burning flesh. His hot mouth closing over me. I gasp when he flicks his tongue over my clit. Hands flying to his head I twist my fingers in his hair. He pulls back from me, looking up at me then.

"Hands above your head, woman," he growls, the sound low in his chest. I nod, following his command and raise my arms back above my head, gripping my own wrists and pinning my arms to the bed.

Theo lowers his mouth to me again. I try my best to keep my arms in place, pinning them to the bed with every ounce of mental strength I have, as he teases me with his tongue.

"You taste amazing, I'm going to stay down here all day, until you're begging me to slide inside you." Theo's lips brush against my inner thigh as he murmurs to me. I smile at the sensation.

I needed this, needed him. How could I have been so blind to it? So blind to him, to us? To the possibility of an us? He has been here taking care of me and I turned him away so easily. Silently I lay beneath his body in my bed, thinking of everything we could have together as he peppers my thighs and hips with kisses, worshiping my body.

"Theo?" I breathe out his name.

"Already? I'm nowhere near done with you yet, Em," he teases me, as he slips a finger inside me and swirls his tongue over my clit.

I toss my head back as a moan escapes me. We go on like this for what seems like hours. My body is tingling and numb at the same time. I need him inside me. I need to feel him slip deep within me and not know where I end, and he begins. My legs begin to shake, and I pray he will finally let me come, will bring me to the edge and push me over it as I lie here panting.

"I need you, Theo."

"Mmm, you have me, Emily," he teases, continuing to finger me as he speaks. Slow steady strokes of my inner walls as I clamp down around him.

"I need you to make me come, please?" I beg.

"Not yet. I want to feel you come when you're wrapped around me and I'm looking into those beautiful, soulful eyes, and I know I am your world." His words shatter my heart. I want to give this to him, want him to see what he needs in my eyes as we make love. But my walls are up, and I don't know how to lower them.

"Fuck me, Theo," I grind out the words at him, trying not to let the anger I am feeling, the frustration that is coursing through me come through in my tone.

I watch as he stands slowly, wiping his mouth with his hand, he is covered with me, covered in my wetness as I writhe on the bed still. He slips his shirt off over his head and unbuttons his pants, sliding them off and revealing himself to me. Hard and ready, the muscles in his chest bunch and smooth as he moves in front of me, then climbing onto the bed on top of me. Slowly he pushes into me, deeper, and deeper. I make to move my arms and wrap them around him but Theo stills.

"Where are those arms supposed to be?" he growls at me.

"Above my head." I still my movement, settling my arms back above my head.

"Good girl," he purrs out the words and starts his steady pace again.

As he pushes into me my entire body tenses.

"You're so wet and ready for me, aren't you, baby?" Theo asks. I simply nod. I do not have the words to respond.

I'm close, so close, and I know that if he keeps up this slow teasing pace I will never get there. I need it hard, rough, faster. I squeeze my eyes closed and will him to move.

"Look at me, Em. I want you to know it is me, only me." As I open my eyes and look into his they fill with something that scares the hell out of me, love. Love from this man is dangerous and I do not want it.

"Fuck it!" he roars, and lifts up on his knees, slipping from inside me.

Taking hold of my hips he flips me, tossing me down onto the bed in front of him on my stomach. My feet scramble for purchase on the carpet and I steady myself, bent over the edge of the bed.

"Is this what you want?" Theo asks as he slams home inside me hard and fast.

"Fuck! Yes!" I cry out. "Fuck me, don't stop, Theo!"

He pistons in and out of my wet pussy the sound of our bodies colliding fills the room and I'm tossed over the edge.

"I'm going to come," I pant.

"Come, come all over my hard cock while I ride you, Em." Theo's words undo me, and I let go of the thin hold I had over my control.

The head of his cock pummels my insides and I explode around him. My hands grip the quilt on the bed.

"That's it, baby, come hard for me. I know you want to. I know you want to come all over me, I want to feel it dripping down my balls as I fuck you." His words push me over the edge again as he reaches around and slides his fingers down over my clit.

Circling it expertly he pushes down, applying just the right amount of pressure and I come again, harder this time, harder than I ever have before. I arch my back and push my ass against his pelvis, pulling him deeper inside me with my inner muscles.

"Goddamnit!" He tenses and steps back from me. "You're going to make me come, woman." I look over my shoulder at him and nod. "On your knees," Theo says and points to the floor in front of him and I do as I'm told, rising from the bed and dropping to my knees in front of him.

As he takes a step forward, I lick my lips, opening my mouth and letting him slide into it. He tastes like me, like my come, he is coated in it. Reaching up I cup his balls and pull on them gently. Twisting them slightly, I look up and watch as he tosses his head back and stares up at the ceiling.

"God help me," he groans. Intertwining his fingers in my hair he pulls me down on him hard and fast, I nearly gag as he hits the back of my throat.

He fucks my mouth then, the same way he did my pussy, hard and fast. I swallow every inch of him that he gives me. I needed this, needed him to use me. When he steps back from me again, I moan out my disappointment at losing the taste of him in my mouth. Theo holds his hand out to me and helps me from the floor, then pushes me roughly against the wall, my breasts pinned against it.

"You want me to fuck you? Want me to take you and make you mine? You don't want soft and loving, promises of the future? You want it hard and fast—"

"Now!" I shout at him, "Fuck me now!"

I stand on my tiptoes, his hand twists in my hair pinning me to the wall and he teases me with his cock, sliding ever so slowly up and down my slit.

Bending forward, he whispers in my ear as he presses the head of his cock to my tight ass hole. "I don't have a condom, Emily. I'm going to fuck you here. I'm going to fill you with my cock and my come and make you mine."

I nod the best I can, pinned against the wall as I am. I want it, I want him buried inside me. I want to feel him explode within me as he fucks me. Pushing forward he is met with my body's natural resistance, I relax around him and let him take me there. Let him push forward into my ass. Hooking a hand under my thigh he lifts one of my legs off the ground, opening me to him more.

"Mmm, yes. You're so fucking tight," he tells me in my ear again as he slides past the barrier and buries himself in my ass. I let out a small whine at the sensation, the small sting of pain and tightness of having him fill me there.

"You wanted this, Em. You wanted me to fuck you hard and rough, didn't you? Like a little slut?"

"Yes!" I pant out the word, willing him to move within me, willing him to continue down this path, knowing all along we can't turn back.

He swells within me then, I look back at him over my shoulder and see the monster I have feared within him, deep in his eyes coming to the surface. He is fighting the shift, fighting his wolf. I don't care. It drives me over the edge, and I push back against him, arching my back and letting him fill me.

"Don't stop," I beg Theo. His hands on me are rough, digging into my scalp and my thigh as he continues to pin me to the wall and fuck my ass.

Grunts fill the room, he pounds forward into me again and again, the wall holding me in place as I turn to putty in his hands. I can tell he is close, his control slipping, it doesn't scare me. Not the way that staring into his eyes and seeing them filled with love for me does. It turns me into a beast, matching his.

"Turn me around," I command. I want to see him. I want to watch him come undone as he fills me. I want to know I have that power over him.

He slips from me then, stepping back, hand on my shoulder he spins me quickly. When he lifts me in his arms with my legs and pushes my back against the wall, I let go of everything I was holding back. I kiss him hard and hungry as he settles me down onto him again. Pinned against the wall, cock filling my ass, I ride him, legs wrapped around his waist, my hands in his hair.

I see the flicker of his control slip away then and he reaches up with one hand, pinning my hands by the wrist to the wall above my head, his strength is astonishing.

"Mine!" He drops his head to my neck and nips at me, I feel the sharpness of his teeth on my skin as he draws blood. Running his tongue up over the sensitive skin there, on the side of my neck, I gasp.

As he pounds forward into me, I'm pushed back against the wall, it scrapes at my shoulders, I don't care. I need this, I've always needed this.

"I'm going to come, Emily. I'm going to fill you with it. You are mine." Nodding at his words I let myself go again and come with him.

Theo rests his head on the wall next to mine for a few moments, then steps backward, taking me with him toward the bed. When he lays me down, he leaves the room and is gone for a short while. Coming back, he brings me a warm washcloth and cleans me up, then crawls onto the bed with me and takes me in his arms.

"I didn't hurt you, did I?" he asks me softly. Looking for my reassurance.

"No." I shake my head. We lie in the dim light filtering in through my still closed curtains for a long while.

"We need to talk about your refusal to let me in," he says sullenly, breaking the silence, breaking the spell.

"You're like a dog with a damned bone." I scowl.

"I'll show you a dog with a bone." He rolls on top of me,

pinning me to the bed and peppering my neck and face with kisses.

I get lost in it. Giggling with him, letting him carry me right over the edge with him into this insanity.

As we lie curled in bed, Theo's arms wrapped around me, I run my fingertips over his knuckles. Noticing for the first time that they are red and bruised.

"What happened?" I ask, turning to look at him over my shoulder.

"I got a little angry last night," he admits and gives me a shy look.

"What does that mean?" I roll over in his arms, facing him directly now.

"I punched a wall," he tells me. The look of shame on his face breaks my heart.

"Why?" I'm baffled at this. Why would he punch a wall? What wall, where, and more importantly, again why?

"When you made me leave. I saw red," Theo admits to me. "I was angry with you." I tense at his words. This is the side of him I was worried about. The side of him that is more wolf than man, as he once told me. The side of him that could hurt me. Not worse than the man who could break my heart, but still a man who could put me in danger whether he meant to or not.

"I'm sorry." I cup his cheek and kiss him gently. "I'm so sorry," I tell him again. I didn't want him to leave at the time and regretted it more and more throughout the night as I spent time with Vince. I knew I would rather have been with Theo.

"Shh, it's okay," he tells me. Kissing me on the forehead.

I roll back to my other side and rest my head on the pillow, letting him wrap his arms around me again and stroke the back of his hand with my fingertips absentmindedly as I wonder about him. About what kind of man he is that could get so angry he would punch a wall. It makes me wonder if he could get angry enough to do that, what else might he do?

As I ponder these thoughts, I slowly drift off to sleep in Theo's arms, wondering to myself, if he is more wolf than man, does that make him more beast than man as well? Does that mean he doesn't have control of his inner monster?

Chapter 8

Theo

I lie in bed with Emily wrapped in my arms, watching her sleep as the day passes around us, forgotten. It is just us here in this moment. Just us together, now, and forever. I was honest with her about what this meant for us. That I would not let her take this back this time. If we moved forward with our relationship, taking it to this level, then that would be it for us.

I don't know how much of that she heard. How much she believed. I don't know if when she wakes, she will tell me to leave and shove the space between us that she keeps forcing on me, forcing the gap between us open wider and wider. I think about all these things as I hold her in my arms, think about having her wrapped around me, about being wrapped around her now and the future. I need to get her to leave this place. To come back home with me where the pack and I can protect her better. I need to put an end to this, whatever it is that is going on. To flush out the man who is threatening her and following her and put an end to him. I resolve to do just that.

Emily

When I wake up, I'm alone in my bed. I can hear the TV in the living room, slowly I get dressed and head that way. Following the smell of coffee and the sounds of him just being in my home. I like the idea of having him here, sharing my space with him. But I still can't let myself lower the walls around my heart for him. I don't know why.

"Hey sleepyhead," Theo calls to me as I enter the living room, scooting over and making room for me on the couch next to him.

"Hey." I kiss him gently on the cheek. Then plop down next to him on the couch. "I was thinking that I was going to invite Clara over to help me rearrange my bedroom, take back the space you know? I mean I've cleaned up everything, but still the idea of someone else being in there when I wasn't home, is grating on me if I am honest."

Theo looks down at me. "No problem. I can get out of your hair this afternoon. I was just sitting here looking at the boards over the broken window and thinking about how I needed to get a new window installed for you. I can head to the hardware store and get everything I need for that project and stay out of your way." I smile at him, at his thoughtfulness and desire to take care of this for me.

"Thank you, but you really don't have to do that."

"It isn't a problem, Em. It needs to be done."

Standing from the couch, I head to the kitchen and pour myself a cup of coffee and call Clara.

"Hey!" she answers the phone excitedly. "How was last night?"

Shit, I completely forgot about my previous night with Vince, our date and then our time here in my place.

"Hush," I tell her. Glancing toward the living room, making sure Theo is out of earshot. "I have a man here."

"Oh Vince? Is that why he didn't come in to work today? He is still there?"

"No," I keep my voice low.

"Emily! You dog you! You have another man there?"

"Yes. I'll explain everything. Do you want to meet me for lunch and then come back here and rearrange my bedroom with me? I just feel like taking the space back, making it mine again after the break-in."

"Sure, but what do you mean? I thought you said they didn't really do anything or take anything." The confusion in her voice is clear.

"I know I said that, but that was because that guy at the bar was listening to us, and I didn't know what to say." I sigh, sipping from my coffee mug.

"You have to tell me everything!" she scolds me.

"I will. I promise! Meet me for lunch?"

"Sure, tacos?"

"Mmm," my stomach growls in response. "Tacos sound great. Meet you in fifteen?"

"Yes! I'll see you there!"

Ending the call, I head back to the living room. "Hey, Theo, I'm going to meet Clara for lunch and then we are going to come back here and rearrange the bedroom. Let me leave you my debit card for the window and supplies you need." I cross the room toward my purse on the table by the front door.

"No need, I'll take care of it."

"No, Theo. I insist." I pull my card from my purse and hand it to him. Not letting him refuse it. "Pin number is 4387. I'll see you later." I lean in and kiss him on the cheek. The moment feels so natural between us. As I pull back, I look into his eyes and see they are sparkling, and he has a smug smile on his face. "Don't fucking look at me like that. It doesn't mean anything."

"Oh, but it does." He winks at me.

I turn to head toward the door, and he pats me on the ass.

"See you later, sweetheart!"

"Don't push your luck there, big guy!" I scowl at him as I leave the house.

"All right! It is time to be honest with me about what the fuck is going on with you, Emily." Clara glares at me over her margarita and I just look back into her eyes. Daring me to speak before I am ready.

"Theo is at my house right now. He came over this morning after I spent the night with Vince." I let the words hang in the air, dropping the bomb on her and watching her for a response.

"Who the hell is Theo?"

"Alaric's brother. My sister's husband, my brother in-law. I met Theo when I went to stay with Sasha before she had the baby."

"You are a dirty girl!" She wiggles her eyebrows at me.

"Shut up!" I glare at her, taking a sip from my own margarita and taking a chip from the basket on the table between us.

"So you called him and he came all the way here to be with you?"

"No, that's not exactly the case. He has been here for a few days. He followed me home."

"What? Like a stalker?" The word stalker stabs a knife right through me, I need to tell her the rest of it. Explain everything to her.

"No, but now that you mention it, I might have a stalker."

"What! What in the actual fuck is going on? You need to start from the beginning and tell me everything, because I feel like I am just getting bits and pieces here and things aren't adding up. Spill it!"

Taking a deep breath, I think back through everything that has happened over the past few weeks, during my time with Theo back at his cabin, our time together there. I think through the entire week I have been home, the break-in, the car that has been following me, the picture, the flowers, all of it rushes through my mind.

I tell Clara everything. Even about being with Vince last night and Theo this morning. It is cathartic to get it all out. It feels incredible to have the weight lifted off my shoulders.

"Wow," she says it quietly, it is all she says for a long while. "Wow, Em."

"You're going to have to give me more than that, Clara," I tell her, picking at the plate of tacos in front of me now.

"I don't know what to say. I really don't. I get why you want to rearrange your house. Like you really do need to reclaim the space as your own. He is there now?"

"Yes," I say and nod.

"Oh goodie! I want to meet him."

"Of course, you do!" I roll my eyes at her.

"Well hurry up and finish eating! Then I can go meet the guy who wants to steal you away from me!"

We finish our meal in silence. I don't have anything more

to say to her and she is clearly just thinking through everything I told her.

"Are you ready?" I ask as we head out of the restaurant.

"Yes!" she nearly squeals at me.

"Okay, I'll see you there, and Clara?" I turn to her as we reach our cars.

"Please don't embarrass me."

Putting her hand on her heart she feigns hurt and looks me dead in the eyes.

She gasps. "Me? Never!"

"Mmmhmm, sure." I glare at her.

I sit across the room and watch as the women eat their lunch. Blending in with my surroundings, going unnoticed. I smile at the thought that they have no idea I am here. No idea I have been here all along. That I will continue to be here.

I glance down at my phone, there is a notification that there is movement detected on one of the cameras I have placed. I smile at that thought. Opening the app connected to the cameras I placed around her house, I scroll through them, and scowl when I see it.

I see the man on the screen clearly, he is in her house. He is there waiting for her to return. It should be me. Should have been me with her there last night and then again, this morning. I watched all of it. Watched it as she proved to me, she is nothing but a slut.

I will change that. I will claim her for my own and show her the error of her ways. When laughter floats across the restaurant toward me I glance over in their direction again. "Soon," I promise her under my breath. "Soon you will be mine."

Emily

. . .

As I pull out of the parking lot onto the main road I look up in my rearview mirror. I see a sedan behind me that makes my heart skip a beat. I feel like I recognize it. Feel like it is the same one that was behind me before.

As I turn, it turns, keeping close behind me. My insides flip, I'm sick to my stomach at the thought of being followed by a stranger. I need to call the police and update them on this. I look again in my rearview mirror as I make the turn onto my road, trying to make out the license plate.

It doesn't follow me, and I can't see the tag. "Shit!" I curse, angry at myself for not thinking of it sooner. It is too late now, since it didn't follow me. Maybe I'm just being paranoid, maybe it isn't following me at all.

I shrug as I pull into the driveway. Clara's car is already parked there. Theo's truck is absent, he must be at the hardware store getting the supplies he needs to fix the window by the front door.

"Where is he?" she asks me as I get out of the car.

"He must have left to go to the hardware store. We can get started." She pouts at me. "Don't worry. He will be back, you'll be able to meet him."

We head for the front door, and I turn at the last second looking down the road where motion has caught my eye. I see what I swear is the same sedan that was behind me on the road before, parked down the street. It is too far away for me to make out the license plate.

"Hey," I turn and say to Clara. "Did you notice that car behind us before?"

"No." She raises an eyebrow at me.

"I'm going to check it out," I tell her as I walk down from the front porch.

"No, Em, don't. I'm sure it is nothing. You're just being paranoid."

I sigh at her words. When I reach the sidewalk the car down the street pulls away from the curb and speeds off.

"Well, okay, I'll give you this. That was weird," Clara says.

"Did you get the plate number?" I turn and ask her.

"No, sorry, Em. I don't think a white sedan is going to be a good description either. There are like thousands of those around."

I sigh again. "I know. Let's go inside. I'll mention it to Theo and see if he thinks we should call the police and give them a description of the car."

"Oh, Theo," she sings his name to me. "You'll ask Theo."

"Shut up." I jab her in the ribs with my elbow as I unlock the front door.

"Sorry. I won't bring him up again," Clara promises. "Let's get started on your bedroom."

Heading down the hall we enter the room, and both look at each other.

"Okay, what are you thinking? I really think the *feng shui* could be much better in here," she teases.

"Oh really?" I ask her, raising an eyebrow.

"Yep." She laughs. "Let's get started. How about we clear off the shelves and the dresser and get those cleaned up, so we can at least have that done before we start moving things?"

"Agreed, you start on the shelves. I'll work on the nightstands."

"Deal."

We work in silence for a while. Moving things off the shelves and nightstands, putting them in piles on the bed and moving some of the larger items out to the living room and placing them gently on the tables and couch out there.

The room is starting to look emptier. When I come back in from setting the lamps on the coffee table Clara is staring at me, holding a picture frame from one of the shelves above my dresser in her hand, she is white as a sheet.

"What's wrong?" I ask her, taking a step into the room.

"Em, you need to call the police."

"What? Why?" I take another step toward her still frozen figure. The picture frame still in her hand.

"There is a camera up here on this shelf, it was behind this frame. Em, it is pointed straight at your bed."

"My bed?" I ask, confused, not processing what she is telling me. "A camera?"

"I bet that is how he got the picture of you in your bed while you were sleeping." She points out the obvious fact that I was clearly missing here.

"Hey ladies!" A deep voice calls from down the hall and I turn just as Theo enters the bedroom. "What's wrong?" He drops the bag he was holding to the floor and rushes to me. Taking me in his arms.

"What's wrong, Em?"

"We found a camera in here," Clara clears her throat and points it out. "I'm Clara by the way."

Theo nods at her as he looks at her over my shoulder. Releasing me from his arms he steps toward her.

"Theo," I say and watch as the two shake hands and when Theo turns his back to her Clara wiggles her eyebrows at me. Of course, even in this moment she is incorrigible and can't stop thinking about sex.

"Don't touch it. Em, do you still have the card for the officers who were here after the break in?" Theo asks me, studying the camera.

"I do." I nod at him.

"Call them, don't touch anything else in here. I'm going to search the rest of the house."

"The rest of the house? You think there are more?" Clara asks the question before I get the chance.

"I think it is a possibility. Call them, Em. Now." His voice is commanding, and I slip my phone from my pocket, turn and head to the kitchen where I have the officer's card pinned to the calendar.

"Shit!" I hear Theo yell from down the hall and rush out of the kitchen, the card and phone still in my hand.

"Call them, now!" he growls at me. "That son of a bitch! I'll fucking kill him." Theo is standing in my bathroom. Confusion fills me, but I can only assume he has found another camera.

"What is it?" I ask, stepping cautiously into the room with the fuming man.

"Call the fucking police, Emily!" he shouts at me.

"Okay! Damn it! I am!" I storm out of the bathroom to the living room and dial the number on the card.

"Jenson?" the man answers the phone on the second ring.

"Officer Jenson! This is Emily Trout. You were here on Tuesday, I had a break-in at my house. We found something that I think you all should come check out. It seems, well... I don't know. But there is a camera."

"Cameras." Theo comes up behind me emphasizing the word.

"Cameras," I correct myself, "in my house."

"Don't touch anything. I will have an officer there momentarily, Ms. Trout."

"Thank you." I disconnect the call and turn to Clara and Theo who are now standing in the living room with me. "They're on the way."

"There is one in the bathroom behind the mirror,

pointed at the shower," Theo tells me and I feel like I am going to be sick.

"Look around out here for anything that looks like it has been moved or is out of place. I want to check and see if there are any more." I nod at his words.

Clara, Theo, and I spread out throughout the living room. Looking behind things on the shelves, and walls.

"I got one," Clara tells us. Theo and I turn to look at her in unison. She is standing by a large photo hanging on the wall above the TV.

Theo goes over and carefully peeks behind the frame, nodding.

I run my hands through my hair. My space feels even more violated now. How can I ever feel safe in my home again?

"Fuck!" I scream out the word. It bubbles up out of me unexpectedly and the shocked looks on my friends' faces tell me they expected it even less.

There is a knock at the door a short while later, as we all sit in silence around the kitchen table. Theo gets up and heads to the front door. I don't budge. I let him lead officer Jenson and his partner into the house and take them back to the bedroom. I can hear their muffled voices as they make their way through the house and finally reappear in the living room.

"This is the last one." Theo points to the wall above the TV and I glance over as the officer's gloved hands remove the camera from its position behind the edge of the frame.

"So, this one is pointed at the front door, the one in the bathroom, and then the third in the bedroom. We will take these back and have them analyzed by the department. We are going to need to get fingerprints on all three of you to rule any of your prints out."

All of us nod at their words. I feel like I'm underwater

watching the whole thing unfold, it seems hazy, and their voices seem far away. I feel like I'm about to have a nervous breakdown.

"We are also going to need statements from each of you. Would you three be able to come to the police station and get this all taken care of this afternoon?"

"I have to work tonight." I speak finally.

"It shouldn't take long, ma'am. An hour or so and then you'll be free to go." I nod at his words.

"Yes, sure. Let me get my purse." Clara and I rise from the table and head to the front door. Both of us grabbing our purses on the way out. I lock the front door and head toward my car.

"I'll drive," Theo offers. I turn to him, the sad look on his face tells me he is worried about me.

I don't know what I look like, but I can tell from the way I feel that he should be and that I don't look good. I nod at him.

Piling into his truck we head for the police station. After we arrive, we each give our fingerprints and our statements. I make sure to mention the flowers that were left on the porch again this morning and the note.

Cursing myself for not thinking of it when we were back at the house and giving them the note that came with the flowers.

"We can send someone over to pick it up this evening," the officer tells me.

"I won't be home. I have to work." I twist my hands together in my lap.

"I'll be there," Theo interrupts our conversation and the officer nods at him.

"Okay good. I will have someone stop by to pick up the card and the flowers. If you notice anything else."

"The car!" Clara shouts all of a sudden.

It is strange how you forget these things when there is so much going on. I completely forgot to mention the car.

"There was a white sedan. We couldn't get the tags on it, but Emily said she thought it was following her, then it showed up on her street. You said this wasn't the first time you have seen it right, Em?" Clara asks and I simply nod.

"Right. I saw it earlier this week. But it is hard to say if it has been following me. I mean it is a white Chevy sedan. How many of those are there in town?" I look at the officer sheepishly.

"No, this is good information to have." He writes down notes in his notepad and looks back up at me. "Is there anything else?"

"No, I think that is everything," I tell him.

"Okay, good. If you think of anything else you have our number. We will send an officer around this evening to pick up the other things from the home. Please be vigilant and if you think of anything else let us know." I nod dismissing his words. Already thinking about having to go home and be in my house again.

"Ready?" Theo holds his hand out to me as he stands and I look over at him, holding back the tears that are threatening my eyes now. "Let's go home," he tells me, helping me up out of the chair and leading me out to his truck parked outside.

Clara leaves as soon as we get back to the house, climbing behind the wheel of her car and making a promise to stop by and see me at work if I need her to. I brush her off. I need to just go and get the day over with. The mundane work of servicing customers and clearing the bar will help to clear my mind and make me feel more at ease.

Theo and I head into the house together. I look around at the disheveled scene we are met with. The things from my bedroom are scattered around the living room. We never finished what we were doing. Everything stopped as soon as we found the first camera.

"I'll get this cleaned up and finish with the room while you're at work. Why don't you get something to eat and then I'll drive you."

"Drive me?" I ask at Theo's final words.

"Yes, I am going to drive you to work and then pick you up. I don't want you going anywhere alone right now." I nod, I can tell from the look in his eyes that he doesn't want to argue, and I honestly don't either. I would feel safer if he were there when I got off.

Chapter 9

EMILY

Theo drops me off at work and I wave goodbye as he pulls out of the parking lot. Then scan it for any signs of the white sedan I have been seeing around town.

Heading into the building I cross through the crowd and settle behind the bar with Katie, she smiles at me.

"Did you have fun last night?" she asks, and I turn to look at her, raising my eyebrow. "Last night, you had a date, that's why you asked me to cover for you?"

"Oh!" I realize now that it was just last night that I went out with Vince. So much has happened in the past twenty-four hours that I can't believe it was so recently. It feels like it has been days. "Yes, I had fun. But I don't think I am going to go out with him again."

"No?" she asks, shrugging.

"No, we didn't really click." I'm honest with her.

"Well, that's a bummer," she tells me. She pauses and

points to the end of the bar, before going on. "I think you have a fan."

"Huh?" I turn, following her gaze and the direction she is pointing. Mr. Whiskey Sour is sitting at my end of the bar. He sends me a small wave.

"Great," I mutter under my breath. Not looking forward to dealing with him and his shit tonight.

"Wanna trade?" Katie offers. "I'll take that side, you take mine?" She is a lifesaver. I tell her so.

"You're a true lifesaver. He has been driving me crazy asking for my number all week."

"No worries. I gotcha, babe." She smiles at me, and we make the necessary adjustments to the bar for us to switch sides. I head over to the customers at the far end of the bar. Settling myself as far from Mr. Whiskey Sour as I can.

The first half of the night is uneventful. I work the bar and keep myself busy. I get a message from Clara checking in on me and shoot her a quick response letting her know I'm good and she doesn't need to stop by.

When I tell Katie I am running to the bathroom for a quick break, I stop by the kitchen and grab some rolls as a snack, then head back to my place at the bar.

I stop dead in my tracks. Mr. Whiskey Sour has moved seats. He is now sitting on my side of the bar. He clearly took the time I was away to rearrange himself and insert himself into my life tonight. Sighing, I head toward Katie.

She glances up at me. "Don't worry, babe. Already made the change." She smiles at me, and I head to the other end of the bar. Positioning myself, yet again, as far away from the stranger as possible. Hoping he will get the message.

I look over at him and he glares at me, the saying, *if looks could kill* comes to mind. I put it out of my thoughts and finish the rest of my shift without much drama. Theo comes into the bar and takes a seat in front of me just before closing time.

"Hey, baby," he calls to me, I smile up at him. "How was your night?"

"Good." I nod and can't stop smiling at him. It feels good to have him here.

She has the nerve to sit there with the mark of another man on her neck. Ignoring me, acting like I do not exist. Playing this game of cat and mouse. She is toying with me. Fucking with me. I do not like it. My anger at her grows throughout the night as she continues to avoid me. I will put an end to this soon. I refuse to let things go on this way any longer.

Slipping my hand into my pocket I bunch the panties still there in my fist. My little piece of her. I've spent the evening not only angry with her for ignoring me, but also for losing the eyes I had in her house. Clearly my cameras had been discovered, I watched the footage of them as they found each one. The feeds died and I no longer have that advantage.

Anger courses through me the longer the night goes on and she avoids me. I wanted to speak with her. Explain to her that we were meant to be together. That the two of us were being drawn together like opposite forces so often are.

Theo

I look at the smile on Emily's face and can't help but return one of my own. It warms my heart when she looks at me this way. When she lets her walls down for a moment and lets me in.

"Are you about ready to go home?" My question and the turn of phrase when I reference her home as ours has a reaction on her and it isn't lost on me.

"Yep. I just need to close out the last couple of tabs before we go."

"All right, I'll just wait. No rush." She nods and turns to finish up what she needs to before we can leave.

A short while later she comes around the bar and stands next to me.

"I'm ready," she tells me, and I climb down from the barstool I am perched on and lead her out of the bar to my truck. Settling her in the passenger seat I turn and make my way around the back of the truck. I stop and scan the wood line, motion there catching my attention.

There is a dark shadow walking along the edge of the woods. A dog maybe, or a wolf. I shake my head to clear my mind. There isn't a pack in this area and there is no reason for any of my pack to be here. I discount what I have seen as nothing. Looking back now and not seeing anything there, I climb into the truck, and we head home.

"I hope you like what I did with the bedroom," I tell Emily as she unlocks the front door.

Looking back over her shoulder at me she smiles. "I'm sure I'll love it."

When we enter the house she freezes, on the kitchen table there is a vase of flowers, battery powered candles sit around the entire room flickering, lighting up the space with a soft glow.

Emily spins to look at me. "Did you do this?" The words catch in her throat, and I realize my mistake. She thinks someone has been in her house again.

"Yes, Em!" I hold my hands out to her, "It's okay. It was

me. I did it. I thought it would be nice for you to come home to a clean house and a warm dinner. I have food in the kitchen, and everything is ready."

"Theo," she coos my name as she steps towards me. "You didn't have to do this."

"I know I didn't. But I wanted to. I wanted to do something nice for you." I open my arms as she steps toward me and take her in them. Wrapping her in my embrace.

"It smells good." She lifts her nose in the air and takes in a deep breath. "Did you cook for me?" she asks softly, setting her purse down on the table by the front door and making her way into the kitchen. "I'm starving! All I had at work was a few rolls."

"I did," I confess as I follow her. "Lasagna is in the oven. Salad is in the fridge. I'll get everything ready. You just sit down and relax." Emily beams at me as she takes a seat at the table.

I head into the kitchen and gather the meal I've prepared, taking it to the table and setting it in front of her.

"This is incredible, Theo," she tells me.

"I told you. I wanted to do something nice for you. You had a rough day." I lean over as I set the salad down in front of her and give her a kiss on the top of her head.

"Thank you." She looks up at me and I can't help myself, I lean down again and kiss her on the mouth. Covering her lips with my own, slipping my tongue between them and intertwining it with hers.

"Mmm," she moans into my mouth. "Will it keep if we put it back in the oven?" she asks me, a sly look on her face.

"I expect it will," I tell her, scooping up the hot pan and slipping it back into the oven before she has the chance to change her mind. "What did you have in mind?" I turn and see her standing next to the kitchen table, her shirt lying on the floor next to her.

Emily takes a step toward me as she reaches behind her back and unhooks her bra, slipping off the straps and dropping it to the floor at her feet. I didn't imagine that lasagna would have such an effect on the woman. I laugh at my own thought, and she tilts her head to the side, questioning me.

"I didn't think that dinner would have this effect on you." I reach toward her and wrap my arms around her waist.

Turning, I take her with me and lift her by the waist, then set her down on the counter in front of me. Stepping between her legs I frame Emily's face with my hands and kiss her. Kiss her the way she needs to be kissed. Claiming her as my mate. I had the forethought to get condoms while I was out today and say a silent thank you to myself for doing so. Emily wraps her arms around my neck and pulls me against her bare chest as I kiss her. I slide my hands up her sides and take her breasts in them.

Gently I twist her nipples between my forefingers and thumbs, and she moans into my mouth. As her nipples harden, and her body comes alive for me beneath my hands, I smile into our kiss. My hands travel, of their own accord, down her sides to her hips and then to the button of her jeans. I quickly unbutton them and lower the zipper. She uses her arms hooked around my neck to steady herself and lifts her ass up off the counter allowing me to slip her pants down over her hips. I pull them down her legs and toss them behind me onto the floor.

Emily sits naked on the kitchen counter. Her hands resting on her thighs. She smiles at me as she slowly slides one hand up her thigh to her waiting pussy and slips her fingers up her slit.

"Damnit, woman," I growl at her. Rushing toward her. "That is mine," I whisper in her ear, and she nods at me. "You can only touch it if I say so." She nods again.

I take a step back from her and smile. Crossing my arms

over my chest I kick a foot backward and lean up against the refrigerator. "Touch yourself for me, Emily. I want to watch you come for me." She smiles then catches her lower lip between her teeth and sends me a sultry look. "Mmm. Tease."

She shrugs but does as she is told and works her fingers over herself. I stand back and continue to watch the beautiful woman sitting on her kitchen counter following my command to pleasure herself while I watch. I get lost in the thought of being with her, inside her, marking her as my mate for eternity. I won't do that to her against her will, won't bind her to myself for an eternity without her say in the matter. But I will do it. Of that, I am sure. She will agree to be my wife and be wed to me.

"What are you thinking about over there?" Emily's voice breaks my daydream of seeing her in a white dress walking down the aisle toward me.

"Being inside you." I wasn't, but the truth would send her running from me. "You begging me to fill you with my cock as I tease you with my mouth again."

Emily closes her eyes and tosses her head back as she continues to rub small circles over her clit. I watch as her thighs tense and I know she is close to her climax.

"What are you thinking about over there?" I return her own question.

"Riding you on the kitchen floor while you suck on my tits." She doesn't miss a beat when she tells me this and she arches her back as she gets ready to come.

Biting her lip, she keeps herself from crying out. But she opens her eyes and looks me straight in mine as she comes. Our eyes locked on each other as she works her fingers over herself riding out the climax.

"So, what's stopping you?" I ask her as I slip my shirt off over my head, unbutton my jeans and step out of them.

I'm rock hard and ready for her. I keep my eyes locked on hers as she looks me up and down. When she licks her lips and crooks a finger at me, I take slow determined steps toward her. Lifting her from the counter when I reach her. Emily wraps her legs around my waist and rubs herself on me. Her wet pussy teasing the head of my cock as I push at her entrance.

"Shit!" she curses in my ear.

"I bought condoms," I reassure her, rubbing my hand up and down her back as I walk her toward the kitchen table.

I set her slowly on it and step back, turning I pick up my pants from the kitchen floor, and slip out the condom I have stashed in the back pocket. Tearing open the package with my teeth, I slide it down over my shaft.

When I turn back to Emily sitting on the kitchen table, she has her legs spread wide, exposing herself to me again. I step toward her and bury myself in her without a second thought. It feels incredible, having her wrapped around me. I need more. I need the friction of slipping in and out of her again and again.

I push inside her further, spreading her inner walls for me as they clamp down around me. "Mmm, you feel amazing," she purrs to me.

"You do," I tell her as I slide from her again, then push forward into her once more.

"Don't stop," she tells me, and I laugh, the sound filling the house.

"Oh, trust me. I don't plan on it." I kiss her then, hard and hungry. It fills my veins with fire, and I need more of her. I need to be deeper within her. I step back from her, and she pouts at me as I slide free of her pussy.

"Don't be sad. I'm just giving you what you wanted." I step back into the kitchen and lie on the cool tile floor.

Placing my arms behind my head, my cock standing straight up in the air, I smile at her, wink and wait.

Emily hops down from the edge of the table and runs toward me quickly, skidding to a stop next to me in the kitchen. She places one foot on each side of my hips and kneels down on top of me, her hand sliding between us, she aligns the head of my cock with her pussy and sinks down onto me.

"God!" I call out, my hands still behind my head. I don't make to move them. I watch her as she bounces on my cock. Smiling at me while she does.

Her breasts bounce with her movement, heavy with their own weight, she is gorgeous, and I could watch her ride me all night. When she leans forward over me and places her hands on the floor above my head her breasts swing in front of my face, and I lick my lips. I watch the perky pink nipples topping her perfectly smooth, pale flesh, as she continues to bounce on top of me.

Lifting my head from my hands I catch her nipple between my teeth and nip at it, hard. Emily sucks in a sharp breath and slams herself down on my cock. My balls slap against her ass as she does. I don't let up the pressure on her nipple caught between my teeth. Instead, I run my tongue in circles around the tip of it.

A moan escapes her, and I watch as she tosses her head back. Each time she lifts herself on her knees and then lowers herself back onto me her nipple tugs between my teeth. She teases herself with her own movements. I smile around her breast still in my mouth as I suck then, pulling her in. She tastes sweet and salty.

Finally, I drop her nipple from my mouth and look up at my handy work, a deep red hickey blooms over her white skin. I smile at my mark then turn my attention to the other breast. Catching the nipple in my mouth the same way, when

I nip her this time, she yelps, but smiles down at me and I don't stop. Don't let up the pressure.

Emily continues to ride me, as I again mark her skin, making her mine for the world to see. Or at least for any man who'd dare touch her. When I pull back, resting my head in my palms again, I look up at my handy work as I watch her. She takes the opportunity to plant her hands on my chest, lifts herself onto the balls of her feet and rides me quickly then. I slip in and out of her. The sound of our bodies colliding fills the space around us. Finally moving my hands, I reach one up and twist it in her hair. Pulling her mouth down to mine. With the other I smack her ass hard and smile, knowing I will be marking her there too.

Her mouth closes over mine and it is her turn to kiss me hard and hungrily. She needs me, I know it. I can feel it in her body. She needs every ounce of this, every ounce of me, of us. I smile into her kiss, and she leans back looking down at me.

"Smug bastard." She glares at me. I laugh at her words and pull her by the hair again.

Kissing her, devouring her, owning her. Heart, body, and soul. She will be mine. She shifts back onto her knees and lowers herself on me. Grinding her clit against my pelvis. I know she is close. She tightens around me, and I feel myself swell within her.

I let her continue her motion, continue the friction on her clit as she rides me. I slide in and out of her quickly as she continues the pace. When she cries out, she stills and I wrap one hand around her hip, the other slipping between our bodies, I find her clit with my thumb and pick the pace back up. I push her hip back and forth forcing her to ride me through her orgasm, rubbing her clit and not letting up on it. I want her to come hard. I want to feel it gush out around me and down my balls onto the floor.

"Fuck! Fuck! Fuck!" she chants the word as she continues to come harder this time.

I laugh, caught up in the moment, in the joy of it.

"Do it one more time for me, Em. One more time, come on. I know you've got it in you." She pants, shaking her head.

Her face red, her body glistening with sweat from the exertion. I nod at her. Then reach up and take both of her nipples between my fingers, twisting them and pulling as I do. She arches her back, slams her ass down on me and drives me home inside her. I lift my hips from the floor and piston in and out of her as she continues her pace.

"Shit! I'm going to come again." She pants.

"I know." I smile at her, not letting up on her nipples or slowing my pace as I fuck her. "Me too."

I can feel myself grow harder inside her as she tenses and squeezes me with her pussy. I let go of her nipples and she falls forward onto my face, I take the opportunity to take her into my mouth again, sucking at her breasts. My hands still on her hips I help her ride me, she is exhausted, I can see it on her face. But I need this. I need her to come for me again so I can come inside her.

"Don't stop," she tells me quietly. I nod my head in agreement.

"I told you. Never." I lick her earlobe and nip her neck. My marks from this morning still there.

"Never," she agrees.

I grab both of her hips and push her down on me again and again as I plant my feet on the floor and lift myself off it, pushing deeper inside her.

"I'm going to come, Em," I tell her just as I feel my balls tighten against my body. I drill up into her one last time and I feel myself jerk inside her and she clamps down around me, we come in unison. Panting, gasping for breath.

When Emily collapses on top of me I can feel her heart racing in her chest. I wrap my arms around her and kiss her on top of the head gently. I want so badly to tell her how I feel, to tell her I love her. My love for her is like nothing else I have ever experienced in this world. In all my hundreds of years I never imagined I could love something this much, someone.

Emily looks up at me, her chin resting on my chest. The look in her eyes tells me she doesn't regret it. Doesn't regret being with me. But still, it is too soon, her walls are starting to weaken but they have yet to fall.

"Time for lasagna?" I ask, smiling at her. She nods at me.

We eat, naked, at the kitchen table. Enjoying the salad and lasagna I fixed for us. It is silent, peaceful. I enjoy the time with her. It feels perfect, like it should always have been this way. When we head to bed it is nearly dawn and I wrap her in my arms and listen to the sound of her breathing change as she falls asleep next to me.

"I love you," I tell her finally. Only once I'm sure she is asleep and won't hear me, won't run from me. But I needed to say it out loud. It was going to burst out of me if I didn't.

Chapter 10

EMILY

I wake to the sound of my phone ringing. I roll over, silencing it. It rings again.

"Hello?" I mumble into the thing, pissed off at whoever dares to disturb me at this hour. Theo's arm is draped over my stomach, and I am enjoying the time here with him. We were up late. It was nearing dawn by the time we finished making love and having dinner together. When we finally fell asleep together in my bed, I was so exhausted my body ached.

"Emily! Vince is dead!" I shoot straight up in bed. The room spins at my sudden movement. Clara's voice comes through the phone as she rushes out her next words.

Theo sits up next to me, his hand on my back.

"He didn't show up to work this morning again and wouldn't answer when we called. They sent the police to his place. Em, he is dead. Someone beat him to death in his apartment the night before last."

There is a knock at my front door, and I look down at the phone in my hand, still trying to process the words that Clara is speaking and now trying to figure out who the hell could be at my door.

"Clara, I have to go. Someone is here," I tell her.

"It's the police. They were here about thirty minutes ago. I told them you were with Vince that night. They said you were probably the last person to see him alive."

"Well, that's not comforting," I tell her as I stand from the bed, throw on some clothes, and head to the front door.

"I've got to go. I'll call you back." I end the call.

I cross the living room and peek out the window Theo replaced on the side of the door. The two officers who were here the other day are standing on my front porch. Cruisers parked behind them in the driveway.

"Hello?" I ask, opening the front door.

"Ms. Trout, do you know a Vincent—he pauses, looking down at his notepad—Walker, Vincent Walker."

"He ain't walkin' no more," the second officer interjects, I turn to him. Shock on my face.

"Ma'am?" the first asks me again.

"Yes, not well. But I knew him. We had a date two nights ago," I confess. I blush, looking over at Theo who is just now emerging from down the hall into the living room. The confession that I was out with another man clearly not phasing him.

"May we come in?" I nod and step aside, letting the officers into the house.

"Coffee?" I ask, as I head to the kitchen to get a pot started.

"No, thank you, we won't take up too much of your time. Where were you around three yesterday morning?" the second officer asks me.

"I was here. Vince and I went to Sweetwater, downtown.

We came back here, hung out and then he left around one."
I shrug, grabbing a mug from the cabinet. "Is he all right?" I
ask, I know what Clara said, but I still need to check.

"No, ma'am, he isn't. Mr. Walker was killed in his
home." I spin and stare at him, unable to believe what he is
telling me. His confirmation of what Clara said is all too
much. I just saw him, less than forty-eight hours ago, he was
here with me.

Theo steps toward me in the kitchen, leading me carefully to the table.

"I'm sorry. I need to sit down." I pull out a chair from the
kitchen table and plop down into it.

"You said he left here around one a.m. What did you do
at that time?" the officer continues, still taking notes on
his pad.

"I went to bed." I shrug.

"Is there anyone who can corroborate that?" he questions
me.

"No, I was alone. You can't possibly think I killed him.
Look at me. He was twice my size." I'm incredulous at the
implication they are making here.

"No, we aren't implying that at all. Just trying to get an
idea of what his last hours looked like."

I nod.

"Did you notice anyone strange while you two were out?
Anyone that he had words with?"

"No, nothing. It was our first date. We had dinner and
then came back here." I shrug again.

"Ma'am, you haven't noticed anyone around since we
spoke last about your break-in, have you? Anyone who seems
to show up at opportune moments. Someone following you?
The list you dropped off at the station and the missing things
from your home, the flowers you mentioned, the cameras.

They indicate that this case is a stalker. We can't rule out that they're related."

"Someone showing up? No." I look around the room for the answers I do not have.

"We will be in touch." The officer closest to me hands me his card as he motions toward the flowers. "Call me if you think of anything." I have a growing pile of these cards here in my kitchen from each time these officers visit.

I nod and watch as they turn to leave.

"So do you want to talk about that?" Theo asks me.

"What about it? The guy I went out with the other night turned up dead this morning. They were here asking about him." He looks at me, turning my words over in his mind. The idea that I was out with another man clearly sticking in his mind even though he didn't seem affected by it moments ago.

"What are you really doing here?" A thought pops into my head and I question him.

"I needed to see you. You texted me yesterday morning, Emily, you initiated this." He looks at me, the hurt in his eyes at my implications hurts me.

I sigh. "Theo, I told you this isn't going to work." I don't know why I am telling him this, just last night I thought about how I shouldn't have sent him away, now he is here and I'm doing it again. I can't help myself. In the light of day, the reality of what he is still scares me.

"Emily," Theo starts.

"Theo, please," I protest. "I need to call Clara. I need to get my mind straight and figure all of this out. The guy I just slept with is dead and now I don't know what that means for me." The words are out before I can stop them and the look of hurt on his face breaks my heart.

When he holds his hand out to me, I notice the bruises

on his knuckles again. I raise an eyebrow at him and step backward away from him. I had noticed them before. Asked him about them even yesterday. It hadn't occurred to me that he was lying.

Someone showing up at opportune moments, someone who has been hanging around. The bruises on his knuckles. Vince being beat to death. It all seems to fall into place.

"Theo?" I ask him, his name coming out as a strangled gasp.

"Emily, it isn't like that. I punched the wall at the motel. I told you that. You asked me to come here. I told you what it would mean if we were together. I was honest with my expectations. Don't do this now. Don't put this space between us again, don't push me away again." I nod at his words, remaining quiet.

"You need to leave," I tell him at last, walking toward the door and opening it.

"Em, please," he asks me.

"No, Theo, you need to leave." Theo steps out onto the porch and I close the door behind him.

I quickly grab my phone from the kitchen table and dial the number on the card the officer handed me.

"Jenson," he answers on the second ring.

"Um, Officer Jenson?" I start. "I think... I... well, I don't know. But you asked about someone hanging around."

"Yes, ma'am, did you think of something?"

"Yes, Theo. Theo has been here. He, well his hands are bruised. I don't know. I don't think—" I'm nearing hysterics as I get the words out.

Theo

. . .

Emily closes the front door in my face, and I push my palms against it. Looking at the bruises on the backs of my hands.

I lost it that night, lost control. I needed her and she wasn't willing to take me. She turned me away again. But then she called me back. We made so much progress. How could she honestly think I was behind all of this? How could she trust me so little?

"Emily," I call her name softly toward the door. Then turn and head to my truck.

I'm almost out of town when I see the lights in my rearview mirror.

"What the hell?" I look down at the speedometer. I'm not going over the speed limit and I haven't done anything that would warrant being pulled over.

Slowing the truck, I pull it to the side of the road.

"Step out of the truck with your hands in the air." The voice comes over the loudspeaker behind me.

When I look up, I see three more cruisers have pulled up behind my truck.

Slowly, with my hands in the air, I get out of the truck and stand, my back to the officers. I could shift and run. I could get myself out of this here and now. But I don't have anything to run from.

As they approach me, I tense, hands still in the air. When they push me over the hood of my truck and proceed to empty my pockets, and then the truck they slam the letter I found on Emily's porch down on the hood in front of me.

"What is this?" one of them asks.

"Shit." I shake my head. I forgot about it until this moment. Forgot to give it to Em to take to the police station with her. "I found that on Emily's porch. She was supposed to give it to the police with the list of missing things from her place." I rush out the words. Praying they will believe me.

"You're going to have to come with us to answer some questions about your whereabouts two nights ago." I nod at them and let them lead me to the cruiser parked behind my truck.

I know after a few questions all of this will be cleared up, and I'll be back on the road by this evening. Then I'll be able to get back over to Emily's and get this straight with her. The thought crosses my mind then, she called them, she tipped them off to me as her suspected stalker and the one who attacked this Vince guy.

The thought hurts my heart, she really doesn't trust me. She truly must be scared of me if she believes me capable of all of this. Maybe I won't go back to her when I'm done with the police. Maybe it is time to tuck my tail and run home.

I smile as I watch the man I have been considering my competition from day one get arrested and hauled off. I took care of the scum that touched her the other night when it was supposed to be our time together.

Now the police have taken care of Theo for me. I look down at the folded picture I hold in my hand. Unfolding it and tracing my fingers over Emily's face on the image.

"Soon, beautiful girl. Soon." I make my promise to her. Placing the picture back in my pocket, I turn and head for her house. "Soon," I tell myself one more time.

Emily

. . .

I consider calling out of work again but decide against it. The distraction of a busy night will be better than sitting at home alone thinking about the past forty-eight hours.

The police called me a few hours ago and told me they had arrested Theo just after he left my house. The letter addressed to me, threatening me, that they found in his truck they say is damning evidence that he was the one who broke into my home. I think it through, he told me about the note he had found on the porch when he was here. Why would he have it still? Was the note the same one he found?

"I just don't believe it," Sasha tells me over the phone as I drive to the bar.

"I don't know what to believe, Sash. He was there, every time something happened, he was there. His hands were bruised. It all adds up. It doesn't make any sense, but it all adds up," I tell her.

"But it isn't Theo. He wouldn't do that, Em. I'm telling you he wouldn't hurt a fly," Sasha continues to insist as I pull up outside of the bar.

"I don't know him like you do, Sasha and I'm thinking maybe you don't know him all that well either." I shrug. "Look, I'm at work. I have to go. I'll call you when I get home."

"Stay safe, Emily. I love you." She ends the call as I head into the building.

The shift goes by pretty uneventful until around eight. That is when Mr. Whiskey Sour takes a seat across the bar from me and smiles up at me.

"Hey beautiful girl," he greets me. I don't give him a second glance. "Hey, don't be like that. I think we got off on the wrong foot. My name is Sebastian," he tells me this with a smile on his face. "You can call me Bash."

"Whiskey sour?" I ask, not acknowledging his words, but having no choice but to serve him still.

"Sure thing." He nods, getting my drift and not going on.

After I place his drink in front of him, I go about the rest of my night as if he isn't there. Refilling his drink as he taps on the glass to signal he needs another. He doesn't push me tonight, neither do the regulars. It is busy even for a Friday night, I keep to myself, just trying to get through my shift. I want to get home to Binx and curl up on the couch with him to process everything that has happened.

My phone buzzes in my pocket and I slip it from my pants, glancing down at the screen fully expecting it to be Sasha checking in on me.

"Tonight."

The message reads. It's from the same unknown number I received the identical message from earlier in the week. Visibly shaken, one of my regulars glances down the bar at me and waves me over. I cross to him.

"Are you all right?" he asks. I shake my head. Not sure if I am.

"I don't think so." I shrug. "I keep getting strange texts. Someone has been following me, and now the person that I thought was responsible is in jail. He couldn't possibly be doing it and I still getting them."

"You're about to shut down for the night, do you want me to walk you to your car?" His offer is a kind one and I nod my agreement. I know that it would make me feel better if I wasn't alone in the dark parking lot.

The question remains, if this isn't Theo, then who is it? I glance suspiciously over at the barstool where Bash was sitting moments ago. It stands empty now.

The entire ride home my nerves are shot. Every set of headlights behind me has me on edge. Everyone and everything seems suspicious. I scan all of the surrounding cars for the white Chevy sedan that we told the cops about. I don't stop watching my surroundings.

I call Sasha about halfway home, not caring about the time. I need to hear her voice. Need to speak to someone about what has been going on.

"Emily?" she answers sleepily. "What's wrong?"

"Nothing. Everything. I don't know, Sash. Something isn't right."

"Alaric is at the police station now. He is bailing Theo out. Do you want me to call him and have them head to your house afterward?" Sasha asks me.

"Yes, please. I don't know how to explain what has been going on," I tell her as I pull into the driveway.

"Theo told us. When he called and talked to Alaric, he told us about the break-in, about Vince. Emily, I'm so sorry. Maybe you should come home with them tomorrow. Come stay here and lie low until the police figure everything out." Her words ignite hope inside me. I brushed off the suggestion before when it came from Theo, but now it makes sense.

"Yes, I'll pack tonight and come back with them tomorrow. It isn't Theo," I tell her as I sit in the driveway.

"I know that," she scolds me.

"No, I'm still getting texts and they can't be from Theo." I head into the house still on the phone with Sasha.

As I enter the living room, I turn on the lights and I'm shocked by the small body lying on the living room floor.

"Binx!" I scream his name.

"Emily! What is it? What is wrong?" I can hear the panic in Sasha's voice.

"It's Binx, he is dead. Sasha! Binx is dead!"

There is blood pooling around him on the floor, he looks like he was attacked by a wild animal. What could have done this?

"I'm calling Alaric. Stay there. They will be on their way. Emily, call the police." She ends the call before I can tell her about Bash, about the guy who has been at the bar night after night. The one who I now suspect has been behind everything.

"Sash?" I call to her, knowing she won't answer. The phone call has already ended.

I sidestep my way around Binx's body and head to my bedroom. I need to be away from the grizzly scene for a moment. Need to catch my breath. When I turn on the light in my room the white lingerie laying on my bed catches my eye and I freeze, hand still on the light switch. The sound of creaking floorboards from the back bedroom makes me turn and peer into the darkness. I'm too late. I should have called the police the moment Sasha ended our call, should have gotten out of the house. He is standing in the doorway looking down the hallway at me. The same eerie smile on his face from each night he sat at the bar.

"Hey beautiful girl," he greets me.

I stand in the darkness of the back bedroom listening to her scream the damned cats name as she enters the house. She deserved it. Deserved to feel the pain I felt having to watch her with Vince and then again with Theo. Stupid slut.

It felt incredible to beat him to a bloody pulp with my bare hands. The cat tasted delicious as I licked his blood from my paws. I watch her silhouette enter the bedroom and my eyes adjust to the light pouring out into the hallway when she flips the switch. She is gorgeous and tonight she will be mine. The icing on the cake was watching Theo be hauled off in handcuffs. Knowing that Alaric and his precious brother would suffer for this.

Three hundred years I was their go to while they stayed with the vampires. Three hundred years, Erik looked over me again and again for advancement in the pack. Then to have to watch the two brothers get exactly what I deserved. The recognition, the welcome home, the women.

It wasn't fair. None of that matters now. Now, I will make Emily mine.

Chapter 11

Theo

I come through the door into the main lobby of the police station and Alaric is standing there in front of me.

"We have to go." He doesn't even say hello before he is on his way out of the front doors and heading to his truck.

"What is it? What's happening?" I ask him, following quickly on his heels.

"Sasha called, someone broke into Emily's house again and killed her cat. She is getting text messages, too. We are supposed to meet her there and then take her back home with us in the morning until the police can figure this out," Alaric continues to speak as he climbs behind the wheel of the truck.

"Someone killed Binx?" The words sound foreign in my ears. Who would do such a thing? Why would anyone do such a thing?

Before I have the chance to ask more questions, Alaric's phone rings. He presses the call button on the steering wheel and Sasha's hysterical voice comes over the speakers in the truck.

"Emily isn't answering her phone. She was supposed to call the police as soon as we hung up. I keep calling her and there is no answer. Something isn't right. I know she is hurt. Someone was there, in the house. Someone killed the cat!" Sasha is rushing out the words. I can hear Alexandria crying in the background.

"You need to calm down, Sash," Alaric tells her. "We are on our way there right now. Hold tight. We will be there in ten minutes. I will have her call you as soon as we get there. I'm sure she is just busy talking with the police."

"Okay. All right. You're right." Sasha starts to calm down.

"We'll call you back. I love you." Alaric disconnects the call and turns to look at me the grave look in his eyes matches my own.

We speed down the road toward Emily's house. As soon as we turn the corner onto her street, I can see the house and I know Sasha was right. Something is wrong. No police cruisers sit in the driveway. No lights come from the windows. The house sits in the darkness, I have no doubt that we will find it empty. Or worse.

I have the spare key to Emily's front door in my hand before Alaric has the truck stopped in the driveway and I am jumping out as he puts it in park.

"Emily!" I scream her name the moment I burst through the front door.

Binx lies dead on the floor in the middle of the living room. I don't bother with the lights, my night vision is better than a human anyway. I don't need the damned lights.

Rushing down the hall to her bedroom I pause. There is a pile of clothes lying on the floor in her doorway. But that isn't what gets me. That isn't what makes me realize my fatal mistake in all of this. It is instead the scent I smell as I take in a deep breath. Wolf. There was a wolf here.

"Theo?" Alaric asks me as I turn and look at him. "Have you ever shifted in Emily's house?"

I shake my head, eyes wide as I stare at my brother standing at the end of the hall. He bends over the body of her dead cat, examining it closely.

"One of us did this." He points to the cat's remains. "I can smell him here."

I simply nod. Squeezing my eyes closed I picture the wolf I saw crossing the yard into the woods the first night I stayed here with Emily after the break-in. What I thought was a wolf that ran out in the street in front of my truck. The scent of him on the bushes the day I found the envelope on the front porch.

"Shit! I fucked up. I fucked this up big time. The signs were all there, Alaric. I should have seen them. Should have known." I close the space between us heading back down the hall to the living room.

"But who would have done this? Why would one of us have done this?" Alaric asks me, shaking his head.

"I don't know. To frame me?" I ask, confusion filling my mind. No other reason makes sense. No other wolves know of Emily and our relationship. Would someone from our pack be out to get me? "Call Dad. Make sure everyone is accounted for. Get the pack together and get them headed here. No, leave some of them behind. What about Sasha? What if they're coming for us all." Alaric nods at my words as he pulls his phone from his pocket.

"Erik!" I hear our father bark on the other side of the phone as the call connects.

"Dad, is the whole pack accounted for? We need you to call a meeting. Get everyone ready for a fight. Something is coming. We don't know what or why, but someone has taken

Emily." Alaric fills him in as I search the house for signs of one of us. For signs of any forced entry.

"Shit!" I hear him yell into the phone and turn to look back at him. "They're all there, except for Bash. He left the day you and Emily did." Alaric is white as a sheet. I didn't know he was gone.

"Bash?" I say his name, not able to compute the information he is giving me. "What would Bash want with Emily?" More pieces fall into place, I tilt my head back, nose in the air and take a deep breath. It is him, it is his scent. I didn't put two and two together before. Why would I? Why would he have been here?

I watch as Alaric nods, then ends the call with our father. "They're on the way," he tells me.

"Do you think Sebastian is responsible for this?" he asks me, just as confused at the idea as I am.

"I really don't know," I tell him, "But it is his scent. It was him who was here. It doesn't make any sense to me though."

As I reenter Emily's room, I find her phone lying on the floor next to her bed. Picking it up I scroll through the call history and text messages. I see one from tonight and another from a few days ago on the screen.

"Tonight."

The word is menacing. A threat in itself.

I think back over the past few days, the first message was from the night I stayed here with her. This one from a few hours ago. As I continue to look through her phone, I decide to give her friend Clara a call.

"Hello, Em? What's up." A sleepy woman's voice comes over the line.

"Clara?" I ask. "It's Theo. Listen, have you heard from her tonight?" I wait for her response.

"From Em? No, why? Is something wrong?" The worry in her voice makes me feel bad for waking her, and worrying her now, but she is the only one who may be able to give us any more information.

"She is missing. We are at her place now. Listen, if I send you a picture can you tell me if you have seen this guy hanging around? If you recognize him at all?" I scroll through my phone looking for a picture of Bash as I continue to talk to Clara on Emily's.

"Sure."

"Okay, sending it now." I hit the send button and wait as I hear Clara take the phone from her ear and push a few buttons on it.

"Oh yea, he was at the bar the other night. Sat next to me. Em said he had been there the night before. Gave off really creepy vibes. Watched her all night."

I nod at Alaric as I continue to listen to Clara's account of the night she was at the bar with Emily.

"Thank you, Clara. I'll keep you updated if we find anything."

"You don't think this has anything to do with Vince, do you? This guy being at the bar then Vince turning up dead? Emily being gone? Do you think this guy is the reason for all of that?" She doesn't let me go. I don't want to hang up on her. I let out a long sigh.

"I don't know, Clara. I really don't know. Thank you for your help. I'll be in touch." I end the call and toss Emily's phone down onto the bed.

"We're never going to find them. We have no idea where Bash would take her, for fuck's sake. We don't even know why." Alaric's words make my head spin.

"I know why. He is jealous. Always has been a jealous piece of shit. He was upset that we were sent to live with the vamps. Then upset when you came back with Sasha, you should have seen the way he looked at Emily the night I got there with her. It ate away at him that he was sent into the woods to find you and then you refused to come back with him. Our father is not an easy man to get along with, he is not one to hand out 'atta boys'. It all makes sense to me. I just don't know where he would have taken her," I finish, lost in thought, racking my brain.

"We will find her, Theo, I promise you. We will find her." I nod at my brother as he speaks. The pack is on its way here.

"We can't track them; he won't be able to take her on foot. Without his scent we won't be able to track them. The only lead we have is that he has to have been the one in the white Chevy sedan that has been following Emily and that isn't a lead at all." I slam my hand against the wall and the photos hanging there shake.

"The pack is coming, Theo, it will be fine."

"They won't be able to track him either!" I spin on Alaric. "We need to call the police and get them involved in this. We need everyone we can get looking for her. I swear, if he hurts her I'll kill him myself."

Alaric nods at me. "I'll call. Sit down for a second." I do as I'm told and head for the couch as Alaric calls the police.

I can hear him in the kitchen relaying the news of Emily's disappearance to them.

"They're not going to do anything," he tells me as he reenters the living room. "They're saying she has to be missing for twenty-four hours before they consider her to be a missing person."

"She could be dead by then!" I yell the words at him, they knock the wind out of me, and I collapse backward onto the couch. "She could be dead by then," I whisper softly this time.

"He isn't going to kill her." Alaric tries to comfort me.

"No, it is going to be worse, so much worse. We both

know what he wants." The defeat in my own voice drives my mood lower.

We sit and wait for the pack, wait for answers, wait for an epiphany that may never come.

Emily

When I come to a sour taste fills my mouth, mixed with the tang of blood on my tongue. I try to sit up, but I can't. As I shift around, I realize not only are my wrists tied behind my back, but my ankles are tied, and I seem to be in the trunk of a car. The sound of the road beneath the car's tires is loud, nearly deafening. I roll to my back the best I can and can see the taillights shining at me, confirming my suspicions that I am in a trunk.

"Help me!" I scream at the top of my lungs. "Help!" I scream until my throat is raw and I finally feel the car start to slow. Hitting bumps as we go, I'm jostled around into the side of the car.

"Shut up!" I hear banging on the top of the trunk above me a few moments after we finally come to a stop.

"Please, let me out of here. Sebastian, Bash! I don't know why you're doing this. I don't even know you. Please. Let me out," I beg the man.

When the trunk pops open and I'm staring into his face the anger I see in his eyes sends fear straight through me.

"You don't know why I'm doing this?" He spits the words at me. "How about because those damned brothers always get all the recognition, all the praise, all the women? While I am subjected to serve them and never get my reward."

"Brothers?" I ask, confusion filling my mind.

"Yes, your precious Theo and Alaric." I freeze at his words.

The memory of the night I first met this man coming back to me. I knew I recognized him when he sat down at the bar across from me at work the first night I was home. I knew he looked familiar, but I couldn't place him. That wasn't the first night we met. We'd met back at Theo's house. He was there. He was one of the guards that went looking for Alaric.

I can't believe I never made the connection, there were phone calls Theo had with Sebastian, he spoke to Sasha. I met him once. It was in passing. But he was there.

"Sebastian?" I turn my head looking at him in a new light now.

"Ah, there it is. There is the light of recognition in those beautiful eyes I was looking for the night I sat down at the bar, and you acted like you had never seen me before. You recognize me now, beautiful girl?"

"But? Why?" I ask, still unable to make sense of this.

"I told you. Those damned brothers get everything in the end, and I'm left to clean up their mess. I wanted you. The moment I saw you, but no. You chased after Theo like a lost puppy the entire time you were there. It is always Theo and Alaric. Always them. It is my turn this time. My turn to get the girl." My eyes go wide at his words.

"We are going to have fun, you and I." He smiles at me then and my skin crawls when he reaches out and brushes against my bare arm. I'm dressed in the lingerie he had laid out on my bed.

"Hush, Em. Don't worry. I'll take good care of you." He bends and trails kisses over my arm following the path his fingers just took.

"Get off of me," I snarl at Bash through gritted teeth, trying to move and get my arm away from him.

"Fine! Have it your way!" Sebastian steps back and slams the trunk closed, hitting my knee. I yelp and jerk back from him as he closes it again, latching it in place this time.

"Help me!" I scream.

"Shut up, bitch!" He bangs on the top of the trunk.

I hear the car's engine start again and feel the road beneath us as we pull back onto it. A long time passes, I scream until my throat is raw and then finally pass out from exhaustion.

Emily

I wake again as the car rolls to a stop. I can hear rocks and gravel crunching beneath the tires. I shift uncomfortably in the trunk, my entire body hurts. My throat is sore from hours of shouting and screaming, all of it for nothing. All of it ignored by the madman behind the wheel.

When he opens the trunk, I see it is dark, the stars in the sky behind him shine brightly, there is no ambient light here and I know we are far from the city. Far from my home.

"Are you going to behave and walk?" he asks me, as he reaches into the trunk for me.

I turn into a wild animal kicking and screaming at the top of my lungs again. I don't want him to touch me, and I'll be damned if I go anywhere with him willingly.

"Scream all you want, no one can hear you out here," Sebastian tells me as he steps back from the car and lets me tire myself out again.

Finally, I stop and glare up at him.

"Let's try this again. Are you going to behave and walk?"

"Fuck you!" I spit the words at him.

"Fine! Have it your way." He disappears from view and when he comes back into my peripheral vision, he has a white cloth in his hand. Pinning it over my nose and mouth I scream and fight him, trying to get him off me. Finally, the darkness wins out and I let my eyes drift closed as the edge of my vision fades.

Chapter 12

Theo

The sun rises on the horizon as we sit on Emily's front porch. The pack arrived just before dawn. Our father stands before me as I pace back and forth in the small space.

"Do we really think Sebastian is behind this?" he asks, not for the first time.

"Yes, it is his scent in the house and around it. I shifted last night and went into the surrounding trees. He has been here for days right under my nose. I saw him more than once but discounted it as nothing. This is my fault. If I had been more aware, more alert, then I could have stopped him before it was too late."

"This isn't your fault," Alaric tells me.

The looks from around the pack say they feel differently.

"We know he is driving a white Chevy sedan. He has been following Emily all week. Leaving her flowers, notes, sending her texts, there were cameras left in her house the day he broke in. Then last night he broke in again, killed her cat and took her. The police won't do anything until she has been missing for twenty-four hours."

"Even with the stalker case they have?" Wyatt asks.

"I don't know. Alaric called them last night. They told him they wouldn't do anything. I'll try to call Officer Jenson directly now and see if I can get a different answer. See if with the case he was building, that they turned against me, if with the cat's death, and everything if there is anything he can do to push things through faster."

The pack nods at me and I turn to go into the house. I find the small pile of cards on the counter next to the calendar and call the one labeled Jenson.

"Jenson?" he answers the phone, a grumpy tone in his voice.

"Officer Jenson, this is Theo. We have met a few times. I am with Emily Trout. We have been working with you this week on her stalker case."

"Ah! Yes, what can I do for you, Sir?" he asks.

"Emily is missing, when she came home last night she was on the phone with her sister, and someone had broken into her house and killed her cat. Then when my brother and I got here she was gone."

"Did you not notify anyone of this previously?"

"Yes! We did, Alaric, my brother, called and he was told that since she hadn't been missing twenty-four hours they wouldn't do anything."

"Goddamnit! We are on the way now, that damned Edwina idiot in teletype, can't get anything right! Mr.... Theo, is it? We are on the way. Stay put, are you still at her house?" I look around the house, my frustration with this entire situation growing.

"Yes, we are here. We will stay put."

"Good, don't touch anything," he instructs me, and I roll my eyes.

"We haven't. The dead cat is still in the damned living room." I catch myself. "I'm sorry. Thank you for doing your job."

I end the call and head back to the front porch.

"Where did they go?" I look at Alaric sitting on the bench on the front porch.

"They shifted, fanned out, and are seeing if they can track him."

"They won't be able to." I sigh as I sit down next to him.

"I know. I told them that." He pats my leg. "Are the police on their way?"

"They are. I talked to that Jenson fella, he is pissed. Says they should be here soon." Alaric nods.

We sit in silence then, neither of us having anything to offer.

"You should call Sasha. Give her an update."

"What update? I don't have anything to tell her. She isn't going to be pleased with that. It's better that I wait and call her when I have something to offer."

"If you don't tell her that we are working on it then she will pack that baby up in the car and drive herself up here." I turn and look at him, raising an eyebrow.

"You're right. I'll call her." Alaric stands from the bench and heads toward the driveway to make his call at the same time as three police cruisers pull onto the street.

I stand, ready to let them into the house and explain what we found when we got here.

"Theo?" Jenson asks as he approaches me. I nod. "I think we owe you an apology for what happened yesterday. Clearly, since she went missing while you were in custody, you're not responsible for this."

"That is what I tried to tell you guys yesterday. Maybe if you had pulled your heads out of your asses and stopped harassing me yesterday then I could have been here to stop this from happening!" I glare at him unapologetically for my outburst.

They all simply nod.

"Did you want to show us the house?" He breaks the silence finally and I turn, opening the front door.

I let them go inside alone, I've seen it. I don't need to see it again. I let them do their work and figure out who did this. Hopefully, this time they can find some answers. Not that we need them. We know who did this, and we will find him, and deal with him our way. My way. I will rip his throat out and kill the son of a bitch for daring to touch my mate. The police don't need to know that. But it drives me batshit crazy that they take so much time in the house. They need to be looking for the car. They need to be out looking for her. Seeing if they can track her down any better than we can.

After what seems like hours they come back. Alaric is sitting next to me on the bench again when they reappear from the house and shake their heads. They're empty handed. They couldn't find a clown at the circus.

"We have the description on the white sedan that was following her. Do you have anything else to give us?"

"I do. We think we know who is behind this. There is a man who has been turning up at the bar every night she has worked. Clara, who you spoke to before, identified him and said she saw him there, and Emily complained that he had been giving her a hard time. I don't think she mentioned it before because she thought he was just another bar fly looking for her number." I stand as I speak, pulling my phone from my pocket.

"I have a photo of him. His name is Sebastian Gordan. We know him actually. He is a member of our…" I pause, looking for the right word. "A member of our circle. He met her once a few weeks back, at my place. We think he followed her here. He has no other reason to be in town, he is from Maryland. He may have taken her back there with him."

"Do you have an address for him? We can send local officers over to check out the place." I nod at Jenson's words and scroll through my phone looking for the address. "We will also need that image. Are you able to text it to me?"

I nod again as I find the address. "I'm sending you the address and the photo now."

"Thank you, Theo. Again, I'm sorry for the misunderstanding yesterday." He reaches out to shake my hand.

"Thank you. Just find her."

"We will." He nods at me and heads down the driveway, his counterparts in tow.

Emily

This time when I come to, I am lying on the ground, it is cold, and smells damp. There is light filtering into the space around me and I turn my head, looking around. I am in what looks like a cave. I realize now the light is coming from a fire not too far from where I am lying on the ground and Sebastian is sitting next to it.

"What are you going to do to me?" I ask him softly, my voice echoes off the stone walls around me.

"Oh good, you're awake." He stands and comes toward me. I try to scoot backward away from him but hit a stone wall.

"Aw, Emily. Don't be like that. I promise you, we will be happy together, you and I. Once you agree to be with me you will see. I will make you my queen." The look of madness in his eyes terrifies me and I swallow hard, tears slip down my cheeks.

"I want to go home," I tell him, the pleading tone in my voice is apparent.

"Soon, baby, soon we will go home." Shaking my head at his words I let the tears fall from my eyes freely.

"To my home," I tell him.

"Ah. Well, that isn't possible."

"You killed Binx," I accuse.

"Hmm, yes. But it had to be done. To punish you for being such a little slut and sleeping with that Vince guy. Then you turned to Theo and fucked him too, like a little bitch in heat. You had to be punished for that."

"You killed Vince." It isn't a question. I know it to be the truth. Know Theo didn't do it. It was all Sebastian, all of it, the entire week, the break-in, the car, flowers, photo, cameras, it was all him.

I was so stupid. I didn't see it. I thought he was just another scum bag at the bar looking for my phone number. I never expected this.

"I did. It was incredible. Bashing his face in with my fists for having the nerve to touch you. Don't worry. I didn't forget about Theo, he will be next, he will be more difficult. But when he comes for you, as he no doubt will, he will be next."

I cry, sobbing then. Knowing what he says to be true. Theo will come, he will hunt me down to the ends of the earth. I heard him last night, as I fell asleep in his arms. I heard him tell me he loved me. I pretended to be asleep. Pretended I didn't hear it. I needed more time. I needed more time to let him in. Then this morning, in the light of day, I was afraid of him. I convinced myself he was behind everything and that it was him whom I needed to fear. I was wrong. God, I was so wrong. The sour taste of regret fills my mouth and I sob harder.

"Hush now. It will be all right," Sabastian tells me. He trails his hand down the side of my face, over my neck stopping at the mark there. "Now this, you will have to be punished for this too. Wearing his marks around in public like they are something to be proud of. You think I didn't recognize it as you ignored me all night at the bar? Didn't recognize it for what it is, his bite? How dare you! You're mine!" He smacks me then and I realize how unhinged he truly is.

My teeth cut into my cheek, and I feel my mouth fill with blood. I don't think for a second that I will be safe with this man, and I pray Theo and the pack find me sooner rather than later.

I wonder briefly if I should try to rationalize with him, but the look he is giving me, the gleam in his eyes at seeing me bleed tells me it would be useless.

"Mmm, Emily. You look gorgeous in that outfit. Don't you like it? I picked it out especially for you."

"I'm cold, if I'm being honest," I confess.

"Oh well let me help you with that. I'll move you closer to the fire." He makes to lift me from the floor, and I tense.

"I can do it. If you untie me. I'll behave. I'll listen and behave now," I beg him. I don't want his hands on me. Don't want to feel his skin against mine. The idea of it alone makes my skin crawl.

"Hmm, and you promise not to run? I'll find you if you do. Wolf, you know. Can track you down and drag you right back here." I nod at his words. I have no doubt he would do just that if I did try to run. The thought hadn't even occurred to me to try it.

"I promise," I say sweetly.

Sebastian moves toward me and works on untying me

slowly, he takes his sweet time. Running his hands up and down my arms as he does. I gag when he gropes my breasts as he works his way over my chest and pulls on the front of the slip I'm wearing, exposing me to him.

He glares down at me, and I tense. I don't know what I have done but the rage in his eyes tells me he is pissed, and that I will pay for it.

"How dare you?" He spits the words at me. My legs and hands having been freed I scramble away from him as quickly as I can.

I'm on my feet and running toward the entrance of the cave before I realize what I'm doing. My fight or flight instinct kicking in and clearly choosing flight. Even though I promised not to run, even though I know he will catch me before I get there, or hunt me down if I escape, I have to try. I can't help myself.

When his hands close around my waist from behind he lifts me from the ground, and I kick the air in front of me, mule kick behind me, trying to catch him in the groin. Meeting only air. I try again and again, the entire way back toward the rear of the cave. I turn into a wild animal in his arms, his strength is apparent as his arms wrapped around me don't budge.

Sebastian throws me to the ground and my head hits the stone floor. My vision goes dark, and I feel like I'm going to vomit.

Theo

"There is nothing here." My father tells me as he crosses Emily's yard toward me.

"I could have told you that. Do you think he took her home? The police are checking it out, but I doubt he would be that stupid. Though, I do think he would head that way, to the mountains where he is more comfortable." I pace the front porch.

"Maybe we should too. See if we can track him down out there. If he has her out there, then he is going to have to shift to hunt. He can't starve her or himself." The pack nods in unison.

"All right, then it is agreed?" Alaric steps in. "We head back home and search that area for her. Let the police do their thing here and if they turn anything up then they will be in touch."

"Sounds like a plan," Wyatt says.

"Agreed. We drove here. So, we will meet you all back there. Let us know if you find anything along the way." I turn to my father. He astounds me then when he reaches for me and takes me in his arms.

"We will find her, son. I will make sure of it. We will find her. She is your mate. I can see that." I'm shocked by his sign of affection, by the gentle way he is speaking to me. Alaric looks at me and smiles. It is clear he is not as shaken by this display from our father as I am.

"Thank you." I step back from his embrace and look at him. "Thank you," I say again, my voice cracking this time. I swallow back the tears at all of this. At finding her only to have her leave me, then to lose her on top of it all.

I had so little time with her, so little time to show her that I was meant to be hers, that we are meant to be together. So little time to love her before things went south. It breaks my heart, all of it.

"Fuck!" I shout out the word. It isn't enough, it doesn't release the frustration and anger I feel building inside me.

The pain of her loss and the hurt at having her gone from me so soon. "Fuck!" I shout it again.

Alaric steps toward me, placing his hand on my back. "We will find her, Theo. We will." As he tells me this, the look in his eyes is one of hurt, and pain. He looks tortured and I wonder if he looks this terrible because of how I must look to him.

I remember how he looked when we were back with the coven, when we were trying to save Sasha, he was a broken man. It is my turn to be broken.

"Let's go," I tell him, turning toward his truck. We will have to stop along the highway on the way out of town and pick mine up where they left it on the side of the road when they arrested me yesterday morning. It feels like that was days ago now.

Theo

By the time we pull up outside of the cabin it is after dark. Sasha is standing on the front steps and runs toward Alaric as he climbs from his truck. I watch the two embrace and it breaks me even more. I put my truck in park and climb out of the cab.

I shift before I hit the wood line. I refuse to sleep until I find her. I head into the dense forest, searching for any sign of them. I make my way in the direction of Sebastian's house. It seems as good a place to start as any to me.

When I finally reach Sebastian's there are police cruisers parked in the driveway. Making my way through the darkness toward the house I creep along the edge of it toward the back door. They're looking through the house, through his belongings, turning the place upside down searching. Good, I think. I don't know what they think they will find. Doubt they will find anything of use. But let them look, let them do their jobs the best they know how and do what they can to find her.

Seeing that there is nothing for me to do here I turn and circle back to the cabin. When I finally make it there, I can hear the others in the woods, the pack is back. They are searching just like me for any sign of Sebastian or Emily. I circle the property, then get an idea and head toward the coven. It is miles from here and it will take me hours to get there, but I wonder if maybe he found somewhere to take her when he was out here with Alaric. I know during that time they spent the majority of their nights in the standing stones. I decide to start there.

As I travel, I watch the moon rise high in the sky and know that it is long past midnight. I continue to watch the moon's path through the sky as it begins to sink on the horizon. By the time I reach the standing stones it is nearly dawn.

Theo, I hear the voice in my mind and turn to see Alaric standing there. I wonder how long he has been following me. Knowing my brother, it has probably been all night.

What are you doing here? he asks. I know this place means something to him. It is the place where he watched Sasha lay on the ground bleeding, all while he thought he was losing everything.

I thought maybe if there was someplace he would take her he might have found it when he was out here with you. Somewhere near here that he would think was safe for him to keep her.

Alaric pauses and looks at me, his face says something, what I am not sure. I twitch my ears as I stare at him.

What is it? I ask, confused at what he is thinking.

There is a place. But if he is there, we will need the pack. I hadn't thought of it before, but there is a cave he followed me to. It isn't far from here. I can't believe I never told you about it. When I was there, I thought... well, I thought I smelled Blake. I thought he had been there. That he had somehow survived that night and made it to the cave before sunrise. There was blood all over the ground. A small camp was set up in the back of the cave.

Blake? I ask. Blake, his other brother. Blake, who was fathered by the same vampire as Alaric, died the night we saved Sasha. We saw it with our own eyes.

Yes. Damn it I had forgotten about it when I got home and Sasha was there. Hadn't thought about it again until just now, but yes, I think Blake might be alive.

Where is the cave? I try to steer him back to the moment, back to the issue at hand and away from the topic of Blake and the impossible idea that he is alive.

I'll take you there. But we need to get the pack first. I don't like it. I don't want to wait.

The more time that passes the more that I have felt that Emily is in grave danger and that there will be a point of no return if we do not act fast.

Go. Get the pack. I'll wait here. I'm not leaving. I fear for her life. I don't want to risk wasting time. If you know where they are going call to them, get them here. Alaric nods and turns from me bursting forward in the direction we came.

I follow suit, my paws hitting the ground with a thud as I turn toward the standing stones. I wait for what feels like hours in the circle. Searching for any sign of Sebastian, any hint of his scent in this area. I make my way to the road and back, following a different path each time. I am feeling hopeless, about to give up when I finally catch it. The scent of him on the leaves covering the ground beneath my paws.

I toss my head back and howl into the night, calling to my brother, my father, my cousins. I have them, I have a lead on them. I quickly follow the path through the woods. Running at full speed.

Chapter 13

EMILY

As I open my eyes, I see him standing above me. I am growing tired of waking with this man standing above me. Tired of seeing his face each time I open my eyes. I am exhausted, my body is sore, and I want nothing to do with Sebastian any longer. I move, realizing I am tied again.

"I'm not falling for it again, bitch. Not only will you be punished for that, but I have decided since you like to bear the marks of a man so much, that I shall give you mine. They will be yours to bear for a lifetime." My eyes go wide.

Sebastian pulls a knife from his back pocket and steps toward me. I scream. I scream as if my life depends on it and that if someone or something doesn't hear me, I will die in the next few moments. Of this I have no doubt.

He takes a determined step toward me, then kneels on the ground over top of me. Pinning me to it beneath his body. Glancing down I notice for the first time that I am completely naked on the ground now.

He straddles me and I cry out again, finally settling into a soft sob. "Sebastian, Bash. Please, you don't have to do this. Please God, don't do this."

"It is too late for that. I tried to play nice with you. You turned me down." He runs the tip of the knife down the side of my face. "You called me a sicko and a sick bastard. Remember?" He tilts his head to the side and sneers at me.

"I didn't mean it. I didn't mean any of it."

"Hush," he tells me as he continues to run the knife down the side of my neck, over my ribcage and across my stomach. "Of course you didn't, and I forgive you. This is to teach you a lesson for running from me. For letting another man mark you. You want to be marked? I'll take care of that, baby. Don't you worry, every time you look in the mirror from now on you will think of me."

At that moment he takes the blade and presses it to the side of my face again, just below my left temple. He doesn't trail it down over my skin softly this time, instead he digs it into the skin, carving me as he goes. I scream bloody murder and don't stop. The knife continues to trail down the side of my neck, over my ribs and down to my hip. He has sliced me all the way down my left side.

I'm screaming still when I hear a howl in the distance. Sebastian and I both go silent at the same moment. I stare up at him, my eyes wide. His are wider than mine. He heard it too. He knows what it means just as well as I do.

He shouldn't be surprised, he told me this would happen. Told me Theo would come. This must be sooner than he expected it. I smile at him, blood's in my mouth and I can feel the hot stickiness of it coating my side and dripping down my body.

I can imagine what I look like, a wicked grin on my face. His plan foiled too soon. Sebastian smacks me hard and I feel more blood in my mouth, the wound on my cheek from my teeth reopening. I gather the blood on my tongue and spit it at him.

"You bitch!" He smacks me again and I continue to smile my mad smile at him.

"You didn't think he would find you this soon. Didn't think he would put an end to your plan before you even got to enact it fully. You're such an idiot to think that. Such a fool to think he wouldn't hunt you down and gut you for doing this. Don't you know I'm his mate?"

As soon as the words slip from my lips I hear the truth in them, it fills my ears and I smile at the memories of Theo and I together that fill my mind. He is right, I am his mate, he is mine. We are meant to be together. I can't believe it took me until this moment to realize it.

"You are not!" Sebastian goes crazy then, stands quickly and rushes to the mouth of the cave. I roll onto my side and wince at the pain in my body as I do. Being sliced open the way I am I know I am losing blood quickly. I can only hope Theo makes it in time.

I watch and wait, as my vision grows hazy, I fight the sleepiness taking me over.

"Theo!" I scream, "I'm here! We are here! Theo!" I keep screaming.

"Shut up you stupid bitch." Sebastian makes his way back toward me, turning his back on the entrance to the cave.

When he reaches me, I am just getting ready to scream again.

"The——" He cuts me off by kicking me in the side.

"I said shut up!" I cough and sputter, blood coming out in little splatters on the stones around me as I do.

"Theo!" I continue to scream. I won't let him silence me. He will have to knock me unconscious before I stop, that, or beat me to death. "Theo! Theo! I'm here! Theo!"

Sebastian gets in my face, the knife in his hand, he makes a deep cut across my cheek, crossing over the cut he already made there, this one perpendicular to the other.

"Theo!" I scream bloody murder. "Theo!" I refuse to stop. Let him cut me to pieces. I will scream until my lungs bleed.

He does continue to cut me, up and down my body, deep horizontal lines coming off the massive one he'd already dealt me. I scream and scream until finally I stop feeling it.

I stare off across the cave, when I see the figure enter, I laugh. I laugh nearly hysterically and Sebastian steps back from me. Looking down at the mad woman he has sliced and diced who is now laughing about it.

"You're going to die," I tell him, spitting blood in his face again.

He kicks me in the side once more and I cough again, I can't breathe, I feel like all the air has been knocked out of my lungs and I will never breathe again.

The roar that fills the cave splinters my ears and Sebastian spins, looking behind himself a moment too late. Theo is on him, taking him to the ground, pinning him beneath his massive paws. I smile at the sight. He came for me. I knew he would. I knew he would find me and put an end to the pain. But I watch in utter horror as Sebastian shifts beneath Theo, throwing him off balance and freeing himself from the wolf.

They circle each other now, each in their wolf forms. Growls and barks fill the air. It is clear they're having a conversation of their own. I can only imagine what is being said between these two men. Both feel they have a right to me.

I start to feel woozy as I watch them, their chests puffed out as they continue this masculine dance of showboating around the cave. I fight the darkness creeping in around the corners of my vision for as long as I can. I see them lunge and snarl at each other. Theo getting the upper ground on some stones, he pounces onto Sebastian. Smiling faintly as he takes him down and takes a bite out of his side. Sebastian yelps. As my vision starts to swim, I see Sebastian roll, getting back to his feet, he launches toward Theo and takes his back leg in his jaws. I scream just as the world goes dark.

Theo

When Sebastian's teeth clamp down around my hind leg, I yelp. Shake my leg and get myself free. I feel blood run down my leg where his teeth tore the flesh. Shaking my head, I clear my mind and spin on him again.

You thought to mark her as your own? Sebastian taunts me again.

You have no claim to her, Bash. She is my mate. Look at her. Look at what you have done to her! That is not love! I shoot back at him as I look at Emily's unconscious form on the ground.

I tire of having this madman in my mind, of hearing his musing about possession and rights to Emily. The sight of what he has done to her makes me sick. I say a silent prayer that the pack will be here soon so I can tend to her wounds. Alaric and I need to heal her soon, she is bleeding badly, and I fear for her life.

Look at me! Sebastian snarls.

I glare into his eyes. They are crazed. I lunge at him, taking him by the side the best I can and throw him to the ground. As he rights himself, he snarls at me.

You will not win this. You will not stop this, Theo. I will not stand by once again and watch you win, while I am passed over again and again.

The smell of blood fills my nostrils as we continue this dance around each other in the cave. I glance back over my shoulder at Emily, my concern for her growing as the scent of her blood permeates the space.

With my back turned for this split-second Bash is on me. He has me by the flank. Teeth cutting through my thick fur and flesh. I turn on him, my lips pulling back over my teeth, revealing them to him. Threatening him again.

How dare you, after all my father has done for you? How dare you, Bash!

His laughter fills my mind.

What has he done for me?

Bash! Stop this now! I try to reason with him over all of this. Try to end this without a fight. He isn't having it. Isn't willing to hear me out and end this peacefully.

I know Alaric and the pack will never make it here in time and I'm losing hope that Emily will wake again. The pool of blood around her on the ground only continues to grow.

It snaps inside me then. I have to end this here and now. I threatened his life, and clearly, he is too far gone to see reason. I will do what I must. I will end this now. I will end him.

Lunging forward I take him by the throat and tear through him with my canines. Refusing to let go, I taste his blood fill my mouth as I do, the hot sticky taste of it is sickening. I don't want any part of him in me. But I do what I must and continue.

Bash shakes from my grasp, I snarl at him as he yelps and moves away from me toward the back of the cave. Toward Emily. I don't trust him there. Don't trust him not to shift and use her against me in this moment.

He does just that. When he shifts, he stumbles toward

Emily's body on the ground. Grabs the knife from the stone floor next to her.

"If I can't have her neither will you!" he shouts at me. Lunging for her. I lunge at the same time and grab him by the calf, dragging him away from her by his leg.

He shifts, but I refuse to let go of him. Refuse to free my grasp on his leg. He turns and snaps at my face, grazing me on the left side. I don't let go of his hind leg as I drag him further from Emily's body. My goal is to get him out of the cave, get him as far from her as I possibly can.

As I drag him into the daylight, he finally escapes my grasp and spins on me. The look in his eyes is that of a man facing defeat. I snarl, pulling my lips back and showing my teeth again. Good, let him see it coming, let him think this is the end. It is.

When he lunges at my side I twist and escape his teeth. Instead, I clamp mine down on his side and tear at the flesh, jerking back in a swift movement as I do, a chunk of his flank comes away from his body with a disturbing crunch. I spit it to the ground and turn to his limp body lying there.

Theo, you don't have to do this, he begs me.

It is too late for that! I snarl back at him. Standing over his body I close my mouth over his throat.

*Theo! No! Please! h*e begs me.

I ignore his pleas and tear at his throat with my teeth. The crunch of bones is music to my ears. His windpipe comes free from his body, and I drop it to the ground at my feet. Looking down at the man I once considered to be as close to myself as a brother, to be a part of my family, I feel a hurt deep in my heart.

His lifeless eyes stare up at the sky as the sun rises above us. I run from him into the cave, shifting along the way. When I reach Emily on the ground at the back of the cave, I bend over her. Reaching my hand out to her neck, I feel for a pulse. It is there, barely there, but it exists. I breathe out a sigh of relief.

"Emily, I'm here. Can you hear me?" I cup her cheek and tilt her head to the side, looking at the cut down her face, her neck, it continues to ooze blood. The smaller cuts perpendicular to the larger one are not as deep, they have stopped bleeding already, surface wounds.

"Emily!" I call to her again. She doesn't respond, but her eyes flutter behind her thin eyelids.

I pull my phone from my pocket and dial Alaric's number. I wait impatiently as the phone rings. He doesn't answer me. I know they are on their way here. It will be hours still before they arrive, it took me hours last night to get here. I slip my phone back in my pocket and look around the space for anything I can use.

I don't have a car here. I came on foot, and I don't know how to get her out of here. I spot a small pile in the far back corner of the cave. Making my way to it I see the pile of stones, the runes carved on them. Someone was here, it all looks so familiar. It is what we used to heal Sasha with the coven. Blake? Maybe Alaric was right, and Blake was here. Maybe he is alive.

I don't have time to process that thought right now, instead I say a silent prayer at having found everything I need to heal her right here. Doing the spell on my own will be tricky, but it is possible. I prepare what I need, setting the stones around Emily's body.

I start the spell slowly, meticulously, working the words over her body. My hands pressed to the wounded flesh. Before my eyes it begins to knit back together. The magic works over her skin, over the wounds, if only it would work on her soul.

I know when she comes to, she will be able to make it out of the cave with me, possibly out of the woods. But she will sleep for days, if not weeks, as her body heals once the initial spurt of energy wears off.

I will have to hurry at that time, carry her if I must. Make my way toward the pack as quickly as possible, so I can get her back to the cabin. It takes time, doing it on my own. More time than it would with my brother, more time than it should. At last, the magic fills the air around us, enveloping her body. The druid spells do their work and I look down at Emily as the magic clears.

She is healed. I grimace at what I see left behind. She is scarred, deeply so. I wonder how deep these scars will go into her heart, her soul. If she will ever be able to forget. If she will ever be able to forgive me for not keeping her safe the way that I promised.

Chapter 14

EMILY

My head feels foggy, my back cold on the hard stone I feel beneath me. I can hear my name being called in the far-off distance of my mind. It is Theo's voice, he is calling to me, but I am sleepy, so sleepy. I feel like I have weights on my arms, legs, and eyelids.

Slowly I move, moaning as I do. I can hear the sound. But it sounds like it is coming from underwater. I continue to hear Theo call my name again and again.

"Emily, Emily, can you hear me, baby? I'm here. Wake up for me." He sounds closer now, not so garbled, like he is moving toward me through space.

"Theo?" I croak out his name, then split my eyelids open with every ounce of strength I have. My vision swims and tips sideways. Quickly, I close my eyes again.

"No, no, Em. Don't leave me. Wake up, sweetheart. I need you to wake up so we can walk." I feel his hand on my cheek, the warm gentle pressure of his palm on my skin soothes me and I turn my face into his hand, smiling slightly. "There she is. There's my girl. Open your eyes and look at me, Em."

I do as he asks and try to open my eyes again.

This time when I do I see his face over mine, his eyes looking down at me, they are full of tears.

"Hey, baby girl." His smile splits into a wide grin and I match it with one of my own.

"Hey," I say softly.

"He is gone. It is over. You don't have to worry about Sebastian again." I nod at his words, not fully understanding or comprehending the meaning of them just yet.

"I want to go home," I tell him, a tear slips down my cheek.

"I'm going to take you home," Theo promises, and I nod gently. "Do you think you can stand for me?" I sit up slowly, taking my time, the room doesn't spin this time as I move. The weights on my arms and legs are still there but feel less heavy now.

"Here," Theo says and stands and takes off his shirt, he bends back down next to me and helps me slip it over my head and get my arms situated in the holes. "Is that better?" Nodding at his question. I do feel somewhat warmer now.

Being on the cold stone floor is not helping. I stretch my legs out in front of me and stand slowly, giving off baby deer vibes as I wobble.

"What happened?" My memories are hazy. I remember being in the trunk of the car, remember refusing to go with Sebastian willingly, then waking up in the cave.

When I tried to run, I hit my head, after that it is only bits and pieces. I can't place the memories in order or bring them fully into view in my mind. I remember blood, lots of blood, the taste of it, the smell of it. Watching the wolves circle each other in the cave.

"I'll tell you everything. But right now, we need to get started walking. It is a long trip back. Can you walk for me?"

"I'm tired. I'm so tired, Theo," I whine.

"I know, the spell does that. I'll let you sleep soon, right now I need you to walk for as long as you can. I'll carry you the rest of the way, but it is time to walk now." He leads me out across the cave toward the mouth of it.

I can see the sun shining brightly at the entrance, lifting my hand I shield my eyes from it's beams. I stumble across the rocks that bite into the soles of my feet and wince at the slight pain there. When I see Bash laying there, his throat torn out, I stop dead in my tracks. Theo's words coming back to me.

"Bash is dead?" I ask, my hand flying to my mouth.

"Yes." He doesn't hesitate on the word.

Theo stares directly into my eyes, every bit the wolf, every bit the beast in this moment. Proud of what he has done. I would like to say that it shocks me, but it doesn't. It makes me beam internally at what this man did for me. I smile at him.

"Good." Flaring my nostrils, I stare down at the body of the deceased wolf. Fighting the urge to kick him. The memories of what he did to me, of what he did to Binx, to Vince, flow through my mind.

Theo leads me down a path away from the cave. We head deeper into the woods.

"If we keep a steady pace, we should make it there before sunset. The pack is on their way here, we should hear them and see signs of them in an hour or two."

"An hour or two? By sunset? I can't walk that far, Theo. I can't do it. I'm so tired."

"I know, baby, come here." He opens his arms to me, and I fall forward into them, needing him to hold me. Needing to tell him so much, to apologize to him for what I did.

I cannot believe I thought he was capable of killing a man over me. I laugh then at the insanity of that thought when the corpse of a man he did kill for me is less than three hundred yards behind us.

"What?" he asks.

Turning my head up, I look at him. "I'm sorry I thought you killed Vince. That you were behind everything. I should have trusted you. Should have let myself trust you. I'm so sorry, Theo. Can you forgive me?"

"Emily, it is me who needs to ask for your forgiveness. It is me who failed you in so many ways. I promised to protect you. I promised I wouldn't let any harm come to you. Wouldn't let anyone hurt you and I failed at that." Closing my eyes as he speaks, I nod.

Theo did make me those promises, but they were ones he shouldn't have made. Ones he had no way of keeping. I shake my head at him.

"This isn't your fault," I tell him, turning and slipping my hand into his. Deciding that we should walk while we talk if we have hours to go yet.

"You couldn't have known it was one of your own behind this. Couldn't have known he would do what he did."

"I could have. I should have. I saw him. But I discounted it as a dog, as something else, anything else. Denial over the idea that anyone in my pack could betray me like that, taking over."

"I saw him too. Or thought I did. But I thought it was you. I thought you were the wolf I kept seeing, I thought you were the one following me. Stalking me. Threatening me. How could I be so stupid?" I asked him. It is exactly how I feel, stupid.

"Emily, what happened last night after you got off the phone with Sasha? What did he do to you?"

I know what he is asking me, I know what images are

running through his mind. I squeeze my eyes closed for a minute.

"It wasn't like that. He didn't hurt me in that way."

I get lost in the memory of it. Put myself back in the doorway of my bedroom when I turned and saw Bash standing there at the end of the hall smiling at me.

"Hey beautiful girl," he told me.

I screamed. I screamed and turned to run. His hand was in my hair before I made it to the end of the hall. Pulling me backward, he made me lose my balance and I fell to my back hitting the hallway floor.

Dragging me by my hair, he pulled me back to the bedroom, my shirt riding up, the carpet burning my back. I gasped for breath, the wind having been knocked out of me when I fell.

Reaching the bedroom, he released me, and I scrambled to my hands and knees on the floor, trying to get away from him. He kicked me in the side then, square in the ribs. I screamed and rolled onto my side. Sebastian collapsed on top of me, stripping my clothes from me.

I was convinced in that moment that he was going to rape me, that he was going to take me then and there against my will. Fighting him with everything I had I clawed at his face, at his clothes. Trying to keep him from getting what he wanted from me.

When the last of my clothes were stripped from my body, I quickly rolled. Shielding his view of me. He stood, blocking the door.

"Get dressed." Sebastian pointed to the lingerie that lay on the bed.

I gawked at him, astonished that he wasn't going to rape me. That he was instructing me to dress for him. Like this was something I was going to model for him. He made me do just that. He made me spin once I was wearing the damned thing. Show him my ass, my breasts pushed up in the cups of the bra.

He stood before me and trailed his fingers down over my skin.

"You're gorgeous. I knew that already. I watched you. You know? I watched you lie in your bed and touch yourself through the window." I winced at his words. I know what night he was talking about and know what he was saying to be true. I had thought I heard him there,

closed the curtains and pushed the possibility of it being true from my mind.

"We will be happy together, Emily. I know you thought of me that night. I know you wanted me to slide inside you and claim you as my own. I will. Soon. I will. Give it time. I want it to be special. To be the right time, in the right place. Slow and steady. Not rushed. We don't have time now. We must go."

"I'm not going anywhere with you. You're a sick bastard!" I grind out the words at him.

"Oh, but you are, Emily. You are." He reassured me that I had no choice in the matter.

I ran then, straight at him, hoping to catch him off guard and slip by him in the doorway. When he grabbed me by the neck and slammed my head against the door frame everything blurred. I collapsed to the floor and stared up at him as he pulled something from his pocket. My mind not making sense of the syringe in his hand at that time.

As I emerge from the memory, telling Theo everything, he stops, pulls me into his arms and holds me tightly against his chest.

"I'm sorry I wasn't there for you. Sorry I didn't stop him." Theo's words break my heart. He would have been there if it wasn't for me.

"If I hadn't called the police on you then you would have been there. This is my fault."

"No! Emily, what he did is not your fault. It is not. Do not think that. Please, never think that." Theo pulls back from me, looking into my eyes. "I'm so sorry you had to go through this."

I nod.

"We need to keep moving. But hang on a moment, I want to check something." He steps back from me and shifts. I watch as he tilts his head back and howls, the sound of it breaking through the quiet woods around us.

It doesn't take long for his call to be answered by the pack, they howl one by one back to him, then in unison.

When Theo shifts back, he looks at me gently. "They're close. You will be able to rest soon."

"I need to rest a while longer now if we can," I tell him gently, hoping he will let me just rest here.

"Sure." Theo scoops me up in his arms and continues walking through the forest without missing a beat.

I start to protest, but I'm too weak, too starved for this man to care. I simply rest my head on his shoulder and let him carry me. The steady rhythm of my head bumping against his chest as I let it loll to the side and his walking quickly, has me feeling sleepier. My eyelids are heavy, and I let them fall, let sleep take me over.

I dream of Sebastian standing over me with a knife as he cuts the side of my face, neck, and body open. I scream, but no one comes.

Theo

I carry Emily in my arms for another mile or so before I see the first sign of the pack. Alaric steps through the woods toward me. His shaggy coat almost red in the sunlight as he breaks through the trees in front of me at full speed. Coming to a stop, skidding on the leaves in front of me, he shifts.

"Holy shit! Theo! What the hell happened?" Alaric pants out the words, his eyes are wide, and bloodshot from lack of sleep over the past forty-eight hours.

"Sebastian is dead." I glare at Alaric, daring him to ask me another question. I'm exhausted, and my goal is to get

Emily back to the cabin safely as quickly as possible. "I'll explain everything to you when we get back to the house."

Alaric nods. Just then the rest of the pack bursts into the clearing we occupy. Skidding to stops all around us, my father, and the others, shift. Voices fill the air around me. I step out of the circle of my family and look over my shoulder at them as they protest. Alaric takes control of the situation and I hear him speaking as I put distance between myself and the rest of the pack.

"Sebastian is dead." The murmurs from the group, tell me not a single one of them has a bit of remorse over Bash's death. No doubt they will split up and head in the direction of the cave to confirm that he is dead and deal with the body.

Alaric comes up on my flank suddenly. I look over at him, and he nods, assuring me that he has handled the situation and that my main focus can be on Emily and getting her home.

We continue our way through the woods. "Are you ready to talk about it?"

"Seriously?" I give him a glare from the corner of my eye. He continues to walk in step next to me, and stares me down. Refusing to budge. I sigh. "I healed her back in the cave."

"How?" Astonishment at my words is clear in his.

"Everything was there, in the cave. It was all there, everything I needed." Alaric wrinkles his brow and looks at me.

"Blake is alive," he insists. I nod. I have little doubt in my mind that he is right in this, Blake is undoubtedly alive. He is the only one who could have been in that cave. The scent of him was there, the stones with the runes on them, all the supplies. It was Blake, I'm sure.

"It seems that way," I tell Alaric.

"Where do you think he is now?" he asks me and I raise an eyebrow at him, the answer to that is obvious to me.

"With the coven. Where else would he be?" I turn to look at him, pausing for just a moment.

"Why would he go back there? That doesn't make any sense." Alaric stops next to me. I continue walking then.

"Why would he need everything to perform the healing spell? He clearly didn't go gather those things and heal himself after we watched him get his throat ripped out. There are too many questions for us to get all the answers without speaking to him." Stepping over a downed log, I shift Emily in my arms. We are getting closer to the house; I can see the sun shifting in the sky and know we should be there soon. "I don't have time to get to the bottom of that right now. I need to take care of Em. I need to get her home and safe and figure out what I am going to say to her when she wakes up, takes a look in the mirror, and asks me how I could let this happen to her."

"Theo, this isn't your fault," Alaric tries to reassure me.

"It is. In more ways than one. This is my fault. I should have been there. I should have fought harder and not let her kick me out that day. Should have made her listen to me. Instead, I left, let her run in the opposite direction from me and call the police. If I had stayed, I would have been there that night. I would have been able to make her see reason in everything and know that this was not me. Then I would have been able to stop him from taking her."

"That is madness. She would have just called the police with you still in the house. In that moment fear won out and she was determined to have you removed from the equation. Right or wrong." Alaric's words grate on me.

"So, you're trying to sell this as Emily's fault?" The growl in my voice comes out as I speak. Angry at his implication.

"That isn't what I'm saying. I'm just trying to prepare

you for the opposite point of view here. For the very real possibility that Emily will blame herself, for this exact reason." I can hear the truth in his words.

"How am I going to do this, Alaric? How am I going to face her when she isn't going to be able to face herself?" I shake my head, the feeling of defeat taking over.

"You don't know that. You don't know what effect this might have on her. She may take it better than you think. Given what she has been through in the past, given that she has watched her own sister be scarred by the fire and branded nearly her entire life. Emily may take this all in stride and surprise you." I hear his words but put little faith in them.

The rest of the trip back to the cabin is in silence. We do reach it just before sunset, like I told Emily we would. I take her inside and cross the house with her, laying her back in my bed where she belongs. I work on cleaning away the blood from her skin and making her as comfortable as I can. I know that the effects of the spell will be working on her now and she will undoubtably sleep for days, if not weeks.

Chapter 15

EMILY

When I wake, I am lying in Theo's bed back in the cabin. I recognize the bedspread and my surroundings. I roll to my side and see him sitting up in bed next to me, his head fallen forward, chin resting on his chest, a soft snore escapes his lips. I smile at the sight.

I reach my hand out and trail my fingers down over his chest, tickling the hair there and sliding lower over his abdomen then back up. I continue to run my hand up and down his body, jumping when he shifts. I look up, he is looking down at me, a smile on his face, his eyes filled with what even a blind man could see is love.

"You're awake." It is a statement.

"I am," I say.

Stretching in the bed next to Theo, I get lost in the wonderful feeling of moving my muscles and enjoy the long stretch. I smile at him as he looks down at me. The love in his eyes is not scaring me as horribly as it has in the past. I trust him, trust he does feel the way his eyes are telling me he does, and he is not just leading me on.

I scoot across the bed toward Theo, stretching out next to him and resting my head on his shoulder. As he wraps his arm around my shoulders and brushes my cheek with his thumb, I sigh.

"I feel like I've slept for days." I yawn, the exhaustion creeping back in already.

"Eighteen days to be exact." Theo's words shock me.

"What?" Sitting up in the bed, I fold my legs under me and look into Theo's eyes. "Eighteen days?"

"Yes, it's a side effect of the spell. It makes you sleep. Don't worry, we have been taking care of everything with the house and the police there." Theo pats my thigh, a soft look in his eyes leaves me feeling uneasy. There is more. Something he isn't saying.

"What spell, Theo? I don't understand." The grogginess of sleep has my mind muddled and what he is saying isn't clicking in my mind. I don't understand what spell he is talking about. Still unable to fathom that I have been asleep for eighteen days.

"To heal you. I had to do a druid spell in the cave in order to heal you. You were injured badly when I arrived, Em." Thinking through his words, sorting through my memories, I try to remember that day in the cave.

To me it feels like it was yesterday, to know it was nearly three weeks ago is something I cannot comprehend right now. I sift through the memories of that day in my mind, pulling each one into focus. One by one, analyzing them as time ticks by. I remember being in the cave, remember hitting my head on the stones.

After that moment they all become blurry, jumbled together, and seemingly senseless. I remember Sebastian with a knife, I remember screaming, tasting blood, spitting it at his face. Blood ran down my face into my eyes. I could feel the sticky warm feeling of it on my neck, my side. But still, none of it makes any sense. Frustrated, I squeeze my eyes closed and try to focus. I am angry with myself for not being able to remember. I feel helpless not being able to make sense of my own mind, my own past unclear to me. Looking up from my lap, I stare into Theo's eyes, and they are full of hurt.

He lifts his hand and traces his fingertips down the left side of my face, over my neck, down across my collarbone, until the neckline of the t-shirt I'm wearing stops him. He isn't telling me something, something he wants to tell me, but isn't, and I can't quite figure out why or what.

"I'm not remembering something. I'm sorry. I'm trying, but it is all hazy. I hit my head and everything after that is muddled, it is blurred together and not making a lot of sense. What happened, Theo? Please tell me." Lifting my hand to his, still hovering next to my face, I push his palm onto my cheek, squeeze my eyes closed and let him infuse me with some of his strength.

"Come here." Theo slowly rises from the bed, standing next to it, holding his hand out to me. As I reach out and take his hand, he helps me to stand and leads me across the bedroom. There is a large full-length mirror hanging on the wall, and it doesn't take me long to realize that is our destination.

Before we reach the mirror, Theo stops me, turns my back to the wall the mirror hangs on and lifts the hem of the oversized t-shirt I'm wrapped in. He lifts it off over my head and I raise my arms, helping him to undress me. I stand before him in only my underwear. Theo takes a deep, steady breath, in and then out. When he squeezes his eyes closed, he places his hands on my shoulders and spins me around.

Slowly pushing me forward toward the mirror, him at my back, hands on my shoulders I see him reflected behind me first before I see anything else. Then I gasp, swallowing hard and trying to keep back the vomit that is threatening me at the vision I see in the mirror. The left side of my face, down my neck, across my collarbone, and across my rib cage all the way to my hip is a deep pink puckered scar. Smaller perpendicular scars intersect it, the one on my face, going from almost my ear to the corner of my mouth.

My hand flies to my mouth now, tears sting my eyes. I'm greeted by the reflection of a horribly scarred woman looking back at me and it shatters my world. This cannot be me; the image of this woman is of a broken, scarred, horribly disfigured woman who has battled to survive. That is not me.

It seems unfathomable that this woman is me.

"Emily?" Theo's voice is deep behind me. His chest pressed to my back I can feel it rumble as he speaks. "Emily, what are you thinking right now? Talk to me, please?"

I don't answer him, instead I let the memories crash into my mind. They do just that, colliding with my consciousness, flooding me with the emotion, the pain, the images of exactly what happened that night. The bits and pieces I was able to see before are now complete. I remember everything, the slicing of the knife down the side of my face. My scream as Sebastian cut me. The feel of the blood oozing from my wounds.

Images of the two wolves circling each other, snapping and snarling, carrying on between them as they circled each other in the cave. Seeing Sebastian pin Theo to the ground, then my screaming and the world went black.

All of it is clear in my mind again. The healing spell Theo had mentioned makes so much more sense now. I must have lost an immense amount of blood. Must have been near death when he was finally able to heal me. I want nothing more than to crawl back into the bed, hide my head under the covers and pretend I don't look this way. Pretend none of this ever happened.

I turn, Theo's hands dropping away from my shoulders. When he stops me, he tilts my head up to face him, his hand holding my chin gently.

"Talk to me, Em."

I don't. I stare through him, not seeing him in front of me, seeing only the images playing through my mind over and over.

Seeing the truth, seeing the scars marking my body, has brought everything back to me. The memories of Sebastian's words about me being marked. The promise from him that I would think of him every time I looked in the mirror for the rest of my life. It is true. I will never be able to forget him. Never be able to put this behind me. Anytime I look at myself I will be reminded of the past.

Even worse, every time Theo looks at me, he will be forced to face what happened again and again. He will never be able to look at me the same again. I will continue to be faced with the soft sadness in his eyes that he pities me for what happened.

As I let all of these realizations fall over me, I collapse into Theo's arms. He lifts me and carries me to the bed. Laying me back on it and resting my head on the pillows. When he pulls the blanket up over my body to my shoulders, I grab it and turn onto my side. Burying my head beneath the blankets as well. I don't want him to look at me. I don't want him to see me. I don't want anyone to see me ever again.

Theo

. . .

I watch Emily roll onto her side as she pulls the blankets up over her head, hiding her face from me. The last thing I see is the look of hatred in her eyes and the tears flowing down her cheeks. My heart hurts, I know what the look means. I know she is hating herself right now. The image of herself in the mirror.

Even worse, I know she is hating me for not being there to stop it, for not preventing this from happening. The walls that I worked so hard to break through to get to her are no doubt back up. I circle the bed, then climb into it behind her. Refusing to let her shut me out. I pull Emily's body to me beneath the covers, dragging her across the bed. Wrapping my arms around her, I slip my head under the blankets just like she has. We have our own makeshift fort and I smile at the thought, but frown immediately when I hear Emily's sobs fill the space around me.

"Emily, roll over and look at me, please?" I rub her shoulders, trying to get her to face me so I can look into her eyes and tell her the truth about how I'm feeling right now. She won't talk to me, but she can still listen.

She doesn't budge, slipping my arm around her waist I pull her against my body, kiss her cheek and brush my lips over her earlobe as I whisper in her ear.

"I will love you no matter what." Making a promise to her. "It doesn't matter to me: the scars, how you look, what happened. What matters to me is if you can forgive me. Can you, Emily? Do you think you will be able to forgive me?" Silence, I'm met with complete silence.

Even the sobbing has stopped, she is simply shutting me out, shutting the world out. Here, under the blankets, Emily can ignore the outside world and what has happened. I squeeze my eyes closed and take a deep breath, in through my nose and out through my mouth. I accept that I will have to set up camp with her here where she wants to hide, in the darkness.

I lie awake long after she falls asleep in my arms, when I roll her over and rest her sleepy head on my shoulder, I brush her hair behind her ear and kiss her cheek.

"I will always love you. No matter what."

"I know," she murmurs in her sleepy voice. "I know."

My heart leaps in my chest, thankful she has spoken, then she is gone again, away in a dreamland where the world isn't so fucked up and she isn't being punished by it. I can't face the other option, that she is in a land of nightmares, wrapped in the darkness she has faced and reliving it again and again. I have no idea how we are going to get past this. What I am going to do to help her overcome the scars, the memories, all of it.

Pulling her close to my body, trying to hold onto her as tightly as I can I wrap my arms around Emily, my woman, my mate. I refuse to let go of her now that I have her back here with me. Refuse to let her leave, I will tie her to my bed if I must, in order to keep her here. If that is what it takes, then that is what it takes. I care little about the repercussions.

I spend the majority of the night making plans to get her to stay. Short of tying her up here, I come up with nothing.

Chapter 16

EMILY

When I wake Theo is in bed with me under the covers, still holding me, and still awake. I look up at him and he smiles at me. It breaks my heart. I don't know how he can look at me this way. I don't know how he can look at me at all. I can't look at myself. I doubt I will ever be able to again. I'm scarred, damaged, will be forever. Sebastian was right, every time I look at myself now, I will think of him. Always think of him and what he did to me.

The unfairness of it is just that, unfair, an injustice done to me. I don't look into Theo's eyes. I can't bear to look into them. Can't bear the love I see there. I don't deserve it. Any of it. He shouldn't worship me the way he does. Shouldn't have me on a pedestal and love me like this. Especially now. I betrayed him. I turned him in to the police as a stalker, as a murderer, which is so much worse. I didn't trust him when we both needed me to and that is what led us here.

I try to roll away from him and he tightens his grasp on me. "You're not going anywhere. Not until you talk to me." I ignore him and squirm free of his grip. I have been asleep for days, weeks, and I need a shower, I need to wash away the memories, if I can.

I slip from the bed and head to the bathroom. When I reach it, I turn on the lights, but avoid looking in the mirror. I don't want to see the remnants of the damage on my skin. Crossing to the shower I turn on the water, all the way to hot, I hope I can scald away some of the pain I am feeling by inflicting some of my own.

After the water warms, I step beneath the spray of it. Gasping at the sensation of the heat on my skin. Tipping my head back I let the water run through my hair and relax into the stinging pain of it. Pain is good. Pain chases away the memories. That thought stops me in my tracks and I look down at the razor sitting on the small corner shelf. Slowly I reach for it. The gleam of the blade calls to me like a siren.

My hand hesitates over the thing for a long while, I consider what I am doing and pull my hand back for a second. Turning to the shampoo bottle, I fill my hand with some and scrub my scalp. My fingers digging into my skin, the tingle of pain from the sensation of my nails biting into me sends a chill down my spine.

I reach for the razor a second time, thinking it through, I need to regain control. I need to make my body my own again. Have control over my own skin. It is a beast wrapped around my soul, an ugly thing that I cannot even bear the sight of. Sebastian's scars have tainted me.

I pull my hand back again and bury it in my hair, pulling at the roots. Trying to steady myself as I rinse the shampoo from my thick curls. As soon as the last of the bubbles flow down the drain I reach one last time for the razor. As I close my palm around the cool metal of the handle it eases my nerves. My breaths come out in quick shallow spurts. My heart races and I feel tears sting the backs of my eyes. I have never before considered such things. Never before thought myself capable. Lifting the thing from the shelf I press the blade to my calf and slowly pull it across my wet skin.

The feel of the metal brushing over my skin, just kissing it as I use the thing to shave away weeks of unkempt hair, I sigh. I run it up my leg again and again, still considering the unthinkable. As I finish with one leg I move to the other, repeating the process, slowly, meticulously I shave myself, pausing at my inner thigh I jerk my wrist and see a speck of blood. A small nick in my skin. There is no pain, only a rush, it is indescribable, like nothing I have ever felt before.

Lifting the blade, with one goal in mind this time, I press it to the inside of my thigh again. Quickly I pull the blade sideways. The line of blood bubbles up from the cut in my skin, it doesn't hurt. That is what I find most shocking. Instead, I feel a rush, an even bigger high. Stars dance in my vision, and I feel free.

Free for the first time since I returned home so many weeks ago. Free for the first time since I saw the car following behind me. The memories of the photos, the cameras, the flowers, Binx's dead body on the floor, Sebastian's face over me as he sliced his blade down the side of my face, all of it fades away. All of it disappears. I lift the blade and press it to my skin again. Then again. Each cut releasing blood from beneath the surface, each drop of it running down my leg, mixing with the water and swirling down the drain takes with it all the pain and the memories from the past. They seem to swirl down the drain with the blood, releasing each of them from my body as I cut.

I'm free, absolved from it all. I take a deep breath and let the steamy air of the shower fill my lungs. Squeezing my eyes closed and seeing only darkness, only the streams of red blood flowing freely. At last, I do not see his face in my mind. At last, I have cleansed myself of him and all he has done. In my haze I turn off the water, slowly step from the shower, grabbing a towel from the rack on the wall I wrap it around myself. When I look down, I notice the drops of blood on the floor at my feet. Panic starts to well up inside me almost instantly at what I have done. At the shame of others finding out the truth of it. I rush to the box of tissues on the counter and grab a handful. Pressing it to my inner thigh to stop the bleeding.

Lowering myself to the edge of the bathtub, I sit and wait for it to stop. The pain I expect to come from the cuts never does. The shame is crushing. However, I don't care. I toss the crumpled tissues in the trashcan and grab another handful. Wiping up the floor quickly, meticulously, ensuring there are no signs left behind.

As I stand and look around the room my eyes glaze over when they pass over the mirror. I still cannot bear to look at myself, my own reflection is my enemy. Tightly I wrap my towel around my body and cross to the door, as I reenter the bedroom I look around. Thanking God that Theo is not here. I trail my fingertips over the top of the dresser, then start opening drawers, looking for clothes. I settle on a pair of gray sweatpants and an oversized t-shirt. They smell like him, smell like home. I squeeze my eyes closed and take in a deep breath as I slip the shirt over my head. It is heavenly. Catching myself I jerk the shirt down over my torso. I can't indulge in these things, or this moment.

As soon as I am dressed, I crawl back into bed and pull the covers over my head, blocking out the light, and the world. A short while later I hear the door open. "I brought you breakfast. You need to eat." Theo's voice floats across the room to me and I roll my eyes. Thankful for the blankets that hide me from his view.

I don't acknowledge his words or his presence in the room. I simply lie in the bed, and continue to shut him out. When I feel his hand on my back I jump, startled by him, not having heard him approach me. The bed dips and he sits down on the edge of it next to me, pulling the blankets back and letting in the light.

"You need to eat. If you don't want to talk about it, if you don't want to talk to me then fine, that is fine for now. But you must eat, Em. You must take care of yourself." I nod slowly at his words, he is right. I can't very well starve myself here in a house full of family. They won't have it and I have no doubt that every single one of them would lock me up in this room if I tried to leave and go back to Ohio now.

Theo stands and I watch his back as he crosses the room, remembering the not so long-ago moments we stole together in this place. Remembering the days he stayed with me in my home and I thought I could let him into my life. Thought once for a passing moment we could make it work. I know now that I was right before. That I could never be with him. That this thing between us is not fate, I am not his mate, this is not love. At most he pities me now. Pities me for how I look, for what I went through at the hands of one of his own.

When Theo brings the tray of breakfast food over to the bed and sets it beside me, I eye the coffee and toast, the smell of bacon and eggs meets my nose and I hear my stomach growl. I eat, I appease him, and I eat. What other option do I have? I consider this as I chew. Death? Death isn't an option. Realistically, I know that. Know I could not take my own life. But what I did in the shower, maybe? But no. I tell myself that was a one off, and I won't do it again. I lift the coffee cup to my lips.

"Can we talk?" Theo asks, I stop with the rim of the mug

pressed to my lips, lower it and glare at him. Did he not just tell me that I didn't have to talk to him, didn't have to talk about it? Now, so soon, he has the gall to ask me to talk. Impatient man that he is. He shrugs and sends me a sheepish look. "Sasha wants to see you."

This doesn't surprise me, I knew this was coming, knew that my sister would be banging down the door the moment she found out I was awake. I'm surprised she wasn't here waiting for me when I got out of the shower. I just look blankly at Theo. I know regardless of what I say Sasha will be in to see me. She will pester me, just like he is, to talk to her. Just like I have refused to do so with him, I will refuse to speak to her. I'm not ready. I don't want to. I'm being petulant, I know. But this is my life and I'll do what I damned well please.

"Okay." Theo stands from the bed. "If you need anything, Em. I'm here." I look away, I can't bear to see the look of sadness in his eyes. Any emotion from him right now is too much.

He leaves the room and before the door is even closed it is opening again. Sasha comes in, Alexandria in her arms.

"Big sis," she sighs out the words. "God, I was so worried. I missed you so much." When she settles onto the bed next to me, she lays the sleeping baby in her arms down between us. I reach out to touch the back of her hand, the tiny fingers curled into a fist. She is so sweet, so innocent. She needs to be protected from the cruelness of the world we live in.

I finish my meal in silence, sip my coffee and watch Sasha sitting on the bed next to me. She hasn't said a word yet, maybe she is searching for the right one. Is there a right one? If there is I have yet to find it in the depths of my mind.

"Do you want to talk about it?" Sasha asks me. Those are

not the right words. I don't move to speak. Just continue to sip my coffee and watch the sleeping baby.

"So, this is how it is going to be now? You're just going to shut us all out?" She is quick to anger, so different from the sadness and pity that Theo has written all over his face. I glance at her and see the redness spreading over her cheeks, she is beyond angry. She is pissed with my refusal to speak. I don't let it get to me, don't let it break through my resolve. "You're not leaving." I expected as much. It doesn't faze me. I have no life to go back to. That version of me is dead, left back in the cave when she was carved up by Sebastian.

"Emily!" Sasha shouts my name and Alexandria jerks awake, her small cry filling the room. I glower at my sister, scoop up the baby and rise from the bed.

Holding this little girl in my arms, this little life infuses me with a strength I hadn't felt moments before. I bounce her in my arms and coo to her softly, settling into a soft hum of a lullaby until she at last falls back asleep as I circle the room.

"Emily," Sasha starts more gently this time, "how long do you think you will be able to keep this up for? Do you remember the summer you were in tenth grade and tried to give me the silent treatment? You lasted two hours." Her look is that of a woman convinced she is right. She is, I did only last two hours before I forgot that I had sworn never to speak to her again and burst into her room with a note from one boy or another at school that I found tucked into my math book. I was so excited to share it with her, so excited to have my little sister to talk to at that moment.

I have nothing to say now, no excitement, nothing to share. Only sadness, only remorse, and hatred. She doesn't deserve that from me. This isn't her fault. Though, if she wasn't who she is, then I would never have met these men. I try, but I can't find it in myself to blame her. To blame anyone but me.

"Em," she tries again. I turn away from her, continuing to carry Alexandria around the room. "Please don't shut me out. Please don't shut Theo out. We need you. We love you."

As I stop in front of the window I look out into the woods, into the world that has betrayed me. I wonder about things: life, pain, love. I wonder about all of it and what any of it actually means. I shake my head then, telling her no. I will not. Not yet. Not now. Maybe never, be ready to speak about the unspeakable.

"Do you want me to leave?" I don't respond. Indifferent to whether she stays or goes. "Okay, when you're ready. I am here. Do you want me to take the baby?" She rises from the bed and steps toward me. I consider it for a long moment and then shake my head.

I settle back onto the bed, resting on the pillows, and lay Alexandria on my chest. Kissing the top of her head I take a deep breath, breathing in the scent of the tiny human who is sleeping soundly in my arms. I give her a soft smile, for her I can manage such things. For her I can be here, present. She is undemanding, doesn't require words, truths I'm not ready to hear. Sasha leaves the room and slowly I drift off to sleep with my niece, praying I won't have the nightmares and have to relive it all again.

Theo

"Anything?" I ask Sasha as soon as she comes out of my bedroom. I notice that she doesn't have Alexandria in her arms and hope fills me that maybe they spoke. Maybe something passed between the sisters and Emily is at least willing to open up to Sasha.

"Nothing." She shakes her head sullenly. "She wanted to keep the baby. They're napping." She points back at the room. "Keep an ear out and let me know when she wakes. I'll need to feed her. I'm going to go get some breakfast myself." I nod and watch her leave.

Settling back into the chair in the living room, eyes trained on the bedroom door for any signs of movement from within. What feels like hours pass, Alaric comes into the room and sits next to me.

"Any change?" I shake my head at his question, letting out a long breath.

"No, she is either still sleeping, or they're awake in there and she is just shutting us out." I shift in my seat, turning to my brother.

"I don't know what to do."

"Give her time," Alaric's words make sense in my mind. But in practice that is so much harder. "She just woke up. Just saw herself for the first time. She needs to process this. Needs to get through what happened to her so she can be herself again."

"Why won't she let me help her though?" Being unable to stand the feeling of helplessness I cover my face with my hands, running them over my stubbled chin, and long hair. The weeks that I have spent at her side while she slept have been long and hard. I have barely eaten, hardly taken care of myself and I know I need a shower, need to show her a wall of strength so she can lean on me in this.

"She is a strong, independent woman who has lived her life on her own. She needs to get through this on her own. She will come to you when she is ready." I wish I could be as sure in this as Alaric is. I am not. "I need to get Alexandria, it's time for her to eat. Do you mind?" Alaric motions toward the door and I nod.

Rising from my chair I cross the room, tap on the door quietly, and crack it open. I see Emily sitting on the edge of the bed, Alexandria resting in her lap.

"Alaric is here for the baby. She needs to eat." I walk across the room holding my arms out to her. Emily rises and comes to me, gently placing her in my grasp.

By the time I return from the hall, handing Alexandria off to Alaric, Emily has already locked herself in the bathroom. I lay back on the bed and watch the door waiting for her to emerge. As time passes, I start to wonder if she is all right, what she could possibly be doing in there all of this time?

I don't hear the shower running, not a sound has come from the other side of that door for what feels like hours. Standing, as panic starts to run through me, I rush to the bathroom door. Pressing my ear to it, then knocking. "Emily! Are you okay?"

Silence, I don't know what else I would have expected. I bang on the door again. There is still no answer. I press my palms to the door, forehead resting against it between them. "Emily!" I shout her name and continue, "Get your ass out here! I need to know you're all right." I hear it then, soft footsteps on the floor. The click of the lock.

She opens the door and glares at me. I step back from her, nearly stumbling, the anger rolling off her confounds me.

"I'm sorry. I needed to know you were alive and not lying dead on the bathroom floor." I try to keep my own growing anger out of my voice, but my patience is wearing thin with this silent treatment having gone on nearly all day. I don't know how much longer I will be able to bear it.

She walks right past me to the bed, pulls back the covers and climbs into it. Ignoring me completely and puts the pillow over her face. I sigh. "Em, please. Don't do this. Don't shut down and block me out. I am begging you." I follow the same path she just took to her side of the bed, kneeling down next to it I pull the edge of the pillow up and look at her face. She has tears in her eyes. "Please, baby. It's me. Don't do this," I plead. She blinks at me, her eyes looking right through me now. I snap, quickly stand, and storm from the room, slamming the door behind myself.

Chapter 17

EMILY

I feel like all I do is sleep and eat. The weeks pass slowly, some crawling by. I get lost in the routine of blocking everyone out. Sasha comes to visit me multiple times a day, Alaric has stopped by his fair share of times, pleading with me to talk to my sister and his brother. It is useless. I'm still not ready. Still can't face them and the building shame inside me along with the building number of cuts along my legs and arms have me hiding more and more.

I have switched to long sleeve shirts now, I keep them pulled down over my forearms, hiding the truth from them all. The only thing getting me through the days is the high I continue to chase. Locking myself in the bathroom again tonight, I sit on the edge of the bathtub, pull out a fresh razor blade and start again.

I watch the blood pool around the cut, trailing my finger over the older ones that have started to heal. When I stand, I hold my arms out and try again to face myself in the mirror.

With the rush taking me over I can do it, then and only then am I able to face my mutilated reflection. I scan my arms with my eyes, holding them out in front of me. Then my eyes hitch over the scar on my left side, and I follow the trail of it up over my body to my face.

When I meet my own eyes in the mirror, I swallow hard. The feeling of the warm blood running down the insides of my arms grounds me in the moment, keeping the memories at bay. There is a knock at the door and the spell is broken, I jump and glare at it. I know it is Theo, we do this each and every time. I am only allowed so much time to be locked away in here. Only so much time before he comes knocking, looking for the reassurance that I am still alive. The fact that he so wholeheartedly believes that one day I will not answer, and he will have to resort to breaking down the door shakes me to my core.

I move toward the box of tissues on the counter, applying pressure to my fresh wounds one by one until they stop oozing and the blood starts to clot. Pulling down the sleeves of my shirt and slipping the waistband of my pants back up over my hips I square my shoulders and prepare to face him yet again.

"I wish you would tell me what it is you are doing in there alone, locked away for hours every day. We can't keep doing this, it has been nearly a month of silence, Em." He opens his arms for me, and I walk past him. Ignoring his request for me to fall into his embrace and let him chase away the darkness.

I don't need him to do it for me. I have found the answers I seek in the thin razorblades I use on myself day in and day out. He does not have the same power that they do now. Maybe he once could. Maybe there was a time when he could chase away the unknown fears of who was stalking me, who was hunting me in the night. I found comfort in him then, found solace in his arms. That time is gone now. I don't think we will ever get it back.

He doesn't storm from the room the way he did before. Doesn't huff and puff and threaten and plead and beg any longer. He simply follows me to the bed, pulls me to him and holds me until I fall asleep. This is our life now.

Theo

She hasn't spoken in nearly four weeks. When she looks at me, she is no longer seeing me, only seeing through me. I am at a loss. I don't know what to do for her. I don't know how to help her at all. Thankfully she still lets me hold her, here in this bed, she will let me pull her body against mine and hold her while she sleeps. Her sleep is that of a tortured woman, she cries out, moans, tosses and turns. I try to soothe her in her sleep, since she won't let me when she is awake.

I kiss her forehead, her eyelids, kiss the tears that seep from the corners of her eyes away. Pulling her more tightly to me. I have asked Alaric about spells, anything we could use to erase the memories for her. He tells me they will only return and make it harder to bear then. And make her resent us for taking her truth from her. I know he is right. But I need answers. I need to know what to do. I need to know what she is doing locked away in the bathroom for hours every day.

Does she sob when she is alone? She hasn't shed a tear in her waking moments in front of me, hasn't broken the façade she put up over her face the morning she looked at herself in the mirror while I held her in my arms and watched her break. She only cries in her sleep, only lets her walls down when she thinks no one can see. I have toyed with the idea of attempting to reach her in her dreams.

It is old magic. Some say it is dark. But druid magic has its way of being what you need in the moment. I don't doubt that she would see it as an intrusion, as a way of me trying to force myself into her mind and heart yet again, as she so often accused me of doing in the past when she put up walls between us. So, I have not done it, not yet. But if this continues, I don't know what other choice I have.

I haven't hunted in weeks, I'm exhausted from lack of sleep, and when she lets me hold her in this form it is all that I have, so I cannot bear to shift and risk her hating me for what I am. What I have brought upon her by what I am. But I feel disconnected, like a man who has lost his way. I have lost one half of myself in Emily and the other in losing my wolf. I debate this again and again as I consider leaving her.

There is a knock on the door, just like there is every night at this time. Alaric and the pack are going to hunt. Going to patrol and they are asking yet again if I will come. I slip my arm from under Emily's body and look at her one last time as I make the decision. Knowing I cannot help her if I am a shell of the man she needs me to be. I make up my mind. When I open the door, I step out into the hall, pulling it closed behind me.

"Let's go," I tell Alaric. The look of shock on his face tells me he never expected me to agree to leave her.

"Are you sure—"

I cut him off before he finished the question. "Don't make me second guess this, or I'll change my mind." Alaric simply nods and leads the way through the cabin to the front door. I follow him out into the night.

The moon is high in the sky, nearly full. It has been over a month since I saw it last on the night I ran through the woods searching for any sign of Emily and Sebastian. It feels good to be under the stars again. I shift and head for the wood line. The wind blows through my fur as I run, I let it invigorate me. I needed this, Alaric was right. I needed to be myself, after so much that has happened, I needed to release the tension in my body and spend the night in the woods hunting.

Emily

As the sun filters through the window, it stains my eyelids red, and I know it is dawn before I even open my eyes. I don't feel Theo's arms around me. While I have shut him out, I have grown so used to waking up in his arms that the cool air at my back feels wrong. It should be his warm chest against my back. I roll and look over to his side of the bed. The sheets are rumpled, but it is empty. There is no sign of him in the room as I sit up and look around.

My heart hurts at the realization that he left me. Tired of me and my silence. I had no doubt he would eventually do just that, but it seems so soon. So, finite. I push the covers back and climb from the bed, heading for the bathroom. My sanctuary. I will do what I must to chase away the pain.

Locking the bathroom door behind me, I settle onto the floor and lean back against the bathtub. Pulling out the razor blade and staring down at my scarred flesh. I'm running out of room. The crisscrossed cuts intersect and cover my inner thighs and forearms. Gently I trail my fingers over them, feeling the raised bumps of the scars forming there. These past few days I have had to cut deeper and deeper to get the rush I'm desperately chasing. The shallow cuts that used to give me such a high don't suffice any longer.

With little unmarked flesh remaining I search for just the right spot. The deeper cuts hurt long after the high has worn off and I am left feeling more than just the shame I have become accustomed to. I hate it. I hate myself. I hate what I have let Sebastian reduce me to. I squeeze my eyes closed and the memories flood my mind. I need to block them out, need to chase them away. Without looking I press the blade to the inside of my wrist and jerk, the motion so natural now.

Resting my head back on the edge of the tub as the blood seeps from the wound, I feel it running down my arm into the palm of my hand. Feel the high seeping into my mind. The images of Sebastian standing over me start to fade. I switch the blade to my other hand, my fingers slick with the blood from my previous cut. Doing the same I cut my other wrist and wait for it to take effect. Wait for the numbness to take me over and dull everything.

The darkness that starts to creep into my mind is something I haven't felt before. Something new that makes me uneasy. When I open my eyes at last, I look down at my arms and see the pools of dark red blood on the floor around me. The blood is dark, so dark, too dark. It is not the bright red blood I am used to seeing. There is so much, it coats my hands. My fingertips tingle as I wiggle them back and forth, blood dripping from them into the pools on the floor.

Panic washes over me and I realize what I have done, realize I have cut too much, too deep. I place my palms on the floor and try to lift myself up. But they slip and I feel my head hit the edge of the bathtub. I land on the tile floor, my head hitting it with a loud thud that shoots stars across my vision. When I try to sit up this time the floor tips up toward me and the room spins. It is too late. I realized too late. I try to scream, but after so much silence I don't know if it is real or just in my mind.

Theo

As soon as I enter the bedroom, I can smell it. It is a smell I am all too familiar with. Blood, Emily's blood. I run to the bathroom door. Banging on it. Nothing. Just like every other day. "Emily!" I wait, bang again, and again. No sounds of movement from inside. I don't wait any longer, I shove my shoulder into the door, and it bursts open, the flimsy lock no match for my weight.

I choke when I see her on the floor, she is pale, too pale, and a puddle of blood surrounds her. This is the second time I have had to see her this way. The second time I have had to check her neck for a pulse. It is there, barely, but there. The faint bump, bump, bump, is under my fingertips. But she is bleeding still, losing too much blood. There is so much blood it coats her arms, her hands, the floor.

"Alaric!" I scream his name. "Alaric!"

I lift her in my arms and make my way out of the bathroom, we leave a trail of blood behind us. I am hoarse from my screaming by the time I reach the hall.

"Alaric!" I call to him again. He runs into the living room and sees me holding Emily, limp in my arms.

"I need everything. We need it now. She is losing blood too fast. I can't stop it!" My words are rushed out, my panic continuing to grow.

Sasha rushes into the room, stops in her tracks looking at her sister's limp body on the couch. She screams, her hands flying to her mouth. Alaric has already left the room. I wrap my hands around each of Emily's wrists trying to stop the flow of blood, it oozes out between my fingers with each beat of her heart.

Seconds tick by like hours. When Alaric reenters the room, he starts laying stones in a circle around the couch. Positioning them just so for the spell. He stands at the back of the couch, while I remain kneeling next to Emily, my hands still on her wrists. We start working the magic over her body. Chanting the words and praying to the Druid Gods to heal Emily's wounds. The entire time I cannot fathom what would bring her to this. That she would be hurt so badly, so deeply, that she felt this was her only way out.

At last, her wounds glow amber splintering out between my fingers, still gripping her tightly. Still trying to stop the flow of blood. As the skin beneath my hands knits itself back together Alaric pauses and checks for a pulse. The sad look in his eyes stops my heart and I feel like my world is collapsing in on me.

My hands go limp, my fingers are numb, the blood coating them is sticky and warm. When I lift them and look down at my palms I am gutted. I was too late. I left her last night, went into the woods to hunt, and this is what I must pay for leaving her. This is the loss I must endure. Long moments pass, Sasha sobs, no one moves. We are all frozen in time, in this moment, I know I will be forever.

Sasha rises after a long while and leaves the room, her sobs following her as she goes. Alaric stands and stares at Emily's body. Just stares and waits. For what, I do not know. But he has a confidence about him I do not feel. I know when we healed Sasha back in the coven's compound she was long past saving, I know the magic works deep within the heart, and soul after the spell is finished. But I have little hope, I have so little hope.

Emily lets out a gasp. I jump to her side, lifting her hand and squeezing it gently. As her eyes flutter open, she looks at me for the first time in weeks, not through me. Her green eyes are glossy, but she meets my gaze and smiles.

"Oh, thank the Gods," Alaric says, heaving out a long sigh.

She doesn't stay conscious for long, her eyes flutter closed, and she is gone again. But she is alive, she is still here with me. We will make it through this together. I lift her and carry her to my bed, setting her gently on the sheets and then heading to the bathroom. When I return with a damp wash-cloth I wipe the blood away from her arms, revealing dozens of cuts along the length of her forearms in various stages of healing.

Some deeper than others, some long faded and just thin scars. I run my hand over my chin as I stare down at them. This has been going on for some time now, that is clear. This is what she has been doing locked away in the bathroom day in and day out. Scarring herself, in what I can only guess is an attempt to reclaim her body as her own.

I stand back and look down at her slight body in the bed, she is wasting away, hardly eating, sleeping for days on end, and hurting herself. This is what my love has been reduced to. I can't bear the sight of her and turn away. Looking out the window. It is not her whom I cannot bear to see. It is my failure to protect her that seeing her reminds me of so strongly that it breaks me inside. Heaving my shoulders, I turn back to her and make to start removing her bloody clothes, as I slip off her shirt I toss it to the ground and move to the sweatpants she is wearing. Slowly I pull them down over her hips and gasp yet again.

The same crisscross of wounds starts at her hips and runs down over both of her inner thighs. Deep, shallow, vertical, horizontal, perpendicular, they make a pattern, but then they don't. She is covered in cuts. I squeeze my eyes closed.

"I'm so sorry, Emily. I am so sorry I failed you. I'm so sorry I let you down, that I wasn't there to save you and that it has come to this." I settle onto the edge of the bed next to her and drop my head into my hands.

Jumping when I feel the brush of fingertips over my cheek. "This isn't your fault." Her voice is small and weak when she continues, "It is mine." Tears fill my eyes and I look over at her. Her head resting on the pillows, she looks so small, frail, helpless. I didn't save her when I should have. Now we have ended up here and I have let her down again. I feel completely at a loss. I push my face into the palm of her hand as she presses it to my cheek. Nuzzling into her hand I let her ease my tension. I won't allow her to continue to blame herself for this, but I will take this stolen moment for now.

"Are you speaking to me now?" My voice is soft, I don't want to scare her away like a frightened animal in the woods.

"Hush." Emily presses her fingertips to my lips silencing me. "I'm sorry. I didn't mean for this to happen. It was an accident. I wasn't…" she swallows hard, "I wasn't trying to leave you."

Nodding at her admission, I believe her, and I thank God for it. I believe after seeing the scars scattered over her body like stars in the sky that she didn't do this intentionally. She has been turning to pain as a release from the emotions she has yet to be able to face. It breaks my heart, but it soothes me as well to know she didn't try to end her own life.

"I know you weren't. We can't keep going on this way. Emily, it's time to talk about it. Time to talk to me." She nods slowly in response. I'm terrified she will shut down again. Shut me out and be lost to me.

"I'm sorry. I'm so sorry." Emily breaks then, she lets the tears she has been holding back fall down her cheeks. They coat her pale skin, drip down over her cheek bones. I lean in and kiss them away.

"Shh. It is okay. You're okay. I'm here, Em. I'm right here." I shift on the bed and pull her into my lap.

"I'm so fucked up. Everything is so fucked up." She sobs into my shoulder, burying her face and hiding from me, from the world, from the reality of her life and what has happened to her.

"Look at me, baby." I lift her chin in my hand, tilting her face up to me. When I lower my head to hers and kiss her lips it is the most incredible feeling. Weeks of being shut out, of this growing space between us have broken me just as much as her.

I slide her down on the bed, positioning my body over hers. The heat of her against my skin, after feeling her so cold before soothes me, eases my mind. She is here, in my arms, alive. Continuing to kiss her deeply I slip my tongue into her mouth and twirl it with hers. Emily sighs and the warm air of her breath fills my mouth, another reminder that she is full of life.

Chapter 18

EMILY

I shift on the bed beneath Theo's body. The weight of him on top of me a reminder that he is real, he is here, I can trust that. I can trust him to get me through this. He takes hold of my wrist and holds it out, revealing my arm, revealing my shame. The crisscross of scars there, exposed in the morning light. Slowly he trails his fingers down over them. The tingling sensation from his touch spreads over my skin.

"Tell me about it. About these." His voice is low, he isn't demanding. He waits patiently, giving me time. I squeeze my eyes closed for a moment.

"I needed to be able to look at myself. I needed to know I had done this to myself. To take back control over my own skin."

Theo nods then, sits back on his knees and runs his hand slowly up my inner thigh with an unspoken question. I sigh at having him touch me like this, so intimate.

"The same. If I was going to be scarred, I was going to

be the one to do it. The rush, the high, the release, it blocked out the pain, blocked out the memories." I swallow hard. "But then I started craving it, craving the pain, the darkness, the blood." Theo nods.

"It was a dangerous road to go down." His words aren't scolding. They're honest, blatantly so.

"I know." I turn my face away from him and bury it in the pillow. Squeezing my eyes closed and trying to block out the shame, the hate, the pain.

"We will find another way."

I nod and take a deep breath.

"I'm sorry I shut you out. I'm sorry for so many things. I don't know how you can still hold on so tightly and not run from me. I don't know how you can ever forgive me."

"Because…" he pauses. "I love you."

My tears flow freely at his words.

"I know that now. I'm sorry it took me so long to believe. I'm sorry I didn't believe it sooner." I still can't bear to look at him.

"Emily, please look at me." Theo gives me time. I sniffle, trying to get myself together.

When I open my eyes and turn my head I see it, the love in his eyes. They're filled with it. The immenseness of the emotion fills me, my heart, my soul.

"I told you. You're my mate. I would do anything for you. No matter the cost. I will now and forever fight to bring you back from the brink. We will get through this, together. Don't shut me out again. Please, I'm begging you. Do not run from me again."

I consider it. I truly do. It would be so much easier to go home and put all of this behind me. To pretend it never happened.

"Theo…"

"Don't say my name that way. I am so sick of hearing

you say my name that way and then shoving this wall up between us." His eyes flash with anger. I lift my hand and press my fingertips to his lips silencing him.

"I'm not. I'm not saying that. I'm simply saying I need time. I need to find a way to cope, to heal, to deal with this in a healthy way. I need to love myself again before I can let myself love you."

"Fair enough. I support that one hundred percent. I want you to be happy and healthy. I only want what is best for you. That is all I have ever wanted. I never could have imagined that any of this would happen. If I could have protected you from it, taken it on myself I would have. If I could kiss away your scars I would." He bends and does just that, starting at my temple and moving his lips down over the side of my face, his tongue trails over my collarbone when he reaches the scars there.

Slowly, he kisses each and every scar on my arms, my ribs, hips, and thighs. "Mmm, you're so gorgeous, Em," Theo whispers in my ear, nipping at the lobe.

I turn my face to his and capture his mouth with mine. Kissing him quickly.

"Theo, fuck me. I need you. I need to know I'm still here. Still alive, can still feel. I need this now. Please?" I beg him, knowing he doesn't like it when I talk this way. Knowing he wants to make love to me. To hold me in his arms and show me how he loves me. I don't need love right now. I need to feel. I need to be in this moment.

Without hesitation he slides his hands down my sides, catching the waistband of my underwear in his curved fingers and pulling them from me. Trailing kisses up the inside of my leg from my ankle to my knee, then my thigh. When he buries his face in my pussy I suck in a sharp breath. The feeling of his unshaven face brushing against my sensitive skin ignites my body and he laps at my clit slowly, teasingly.

I groan, as he slips a finger inside me, then another, spreading them and sliding them up and down my inner walls. Coaxing me to life beneath him. He works his tongue over me, and I arch my back. Writhing beneath him. He doesn't stop his motion.

Closing his mouth over me he nips at my clit and the pain shoots through me. When he follows it with a teasing lick up my slit, he slips his fingers from inside me. Then fills me again, stretching me wider this time, three fingers fill me, and he finds my most inner spot. Brushing his fingers against it gently at first as he returns his mouth to my clit.

I moan out his name, "Theo."

He nips me again and I arch my back. I'm close, so close to coming that I'm panting. I gasp and squeeze my eyes closed, stars swim in my vision.

"Come for me, Emily," he commands as he grazes his teeth over me and pounds his fingers into me. Fucking my pussy with his hand. Hard and fast, the way I asked.

I fall over the edge into it. Hands gripping the bed sheets. Theo reaches up and cups my breast, twisting a nipple between his fingers and I cry out.

That is all it takes, and I buck against him. "Good girl," he purrs against my skin.

"On your knees," he tells me as he lifts his mouth from me. When I turn over onto my belly and rise to my knees, he smacks my ass. I let out a small yelp.

My arms and legs are shaky, I'm so exhausted I can hardly hold myself up. I know from the past that the spell will make me sleep, for weeks, and I can't give in to that now. I need to feel him inside me, I need to feel alive, and know that I am still here.

Theo stands from the bed and looks at me, I wobble, and

he tilts his head to the side then shakes it. I know what he is thinking. He is going to deny me what I need. He is going to put an end to this. I try my best to hold myself up, but when I collapse onto the sheets I'm gasping for breath and hardly able to hold my eyes open.

"You need to rest. You died, Emily. The spell is still working its magic and you need to sleep." Theo climbs onto the bed and takes me in his arms. "I'll be here when you wake up."

I shake my head and whine. "I don't want to. I need this," I protest.

"No." The word has a finality about it that leaves me feeling angry. "You need to sleep. Come here." Pulling me to his chest he rests my head on his shoulder and I yawn. My body is a traitor to my mind.

"Sleep." The word sounds different in my mind, it does something to me and I try to fight it but simply cannot, the cloak of sleep takes me, and I fall into it.

Theo

The moment I say the word, laced in the spell she is asleep in my arms. She needs it, needs to rest, and recover. I shouldn't have taken it as far as I did. She needs to heal, I let my own need for her blur my judgment.

Hours pass as I hold her. I watch the sun shift across the floor of the bedroom. When there is a soft knock at the door I slip from beneath Emily and leave her curled in the bed as I go to answer it.

"Is she asleep?" Sasha asks, her eyes red rimmed and full of tears. I nod. But step back and let her enter the room.

I watch as she crosses it and climbs into the bed with her sister. Curling her arms around her and holding her. I forgot that she suffered a huge loss today, too. Thought she lost the last of her family in a moment so dark that it will no doubt haunt her dreams for years. Leaving the room, I pull the door closed behind me and enter the living room.

Alaric is sitting on the couch, the remnants of our spell still scattered around the room.

"Is she all right?" he asks me.

"She will be. She is alive." I shrug. "I can't say much as for her mental state. She did say it was an accident."

"Do you believe her?" He shifts, skepticism fills his eyes.

"I do." I nod. "She has been cutting herself, her body is covered with the proof of that. I think she took it too far this time."

"Shit," he says the word under his breath. "What do you need?"

"Time, time to heal her. Time to convince her she is not damaged goods."

"You have an eternity." He is right in this. I do. But Emily does not. Time here is precious for her.

"Only if I can get her to agree to the spell." I'm not hopeful of that. I have no doubt she will refuse me. But I will wait and when she wakes, I will ask her to bind herself to me as my mate and give me an eternity to make it better for her. "I'll ask. I'll demand if I must. But I will not take the choice from her."

"I know. She will agree."

"To live with me, scarred, marked as she is for an eternity? I doubt it." I shake my head. "I will ask, nevertheless."

"How are you?" he asks me then.

"I'd kill him again if I could. I'd kill him every day for the rest of my time if I was able to do so." The rage I have inside me for Sebastian will never fade, it will not dampen as time passes. I will hate him until my dying day for what he did to her. For what he reduced her to.

"You need to sleep too," Alaric, so full of wisdom informs me. I glare at him. "She will sleep for longer this time. Expect a month at least. You need to rest. You cannot sit awake by her side through all of that. You need to take care of yourself, brother." His words sting, I had planned to do just that. But he is right.

"Sasha is with her now." I use this as my excuse.

"I'll get her." He makes to rise from the couch, I catch his shoulder with my hand.

"No, let her stay with her. I will have weeks to sleep. I am fine here for now." Alaric lowers himself back down next to me.

"Then can we talk about something else?" He shifts the conversation, and I can tell from the tone in his voice that he wants to talk about Blake.

"He is alive," I tell him, confirming his suspicion and my own.

"He is. I am sure of it now. After you found the things in the cave it all adds up. He must have made it there before dawn and been able to heal himself."

"But why the stones? He couldn't do the spell on himself," I point out the obvious.

"No, that is the part that gets me. But he is the only one who could have been there and had everything. It doesn't make sense. I don't have all the pieces yet. But I am going to go to the coven and look for him."

"You can't, Alaric, they will kill you on sight," I protest.

"They may, but I have to know, and I don't know what other way to check."

"They know you are not one of them. They know who and what you really are. You cannot trust them." Unable to make sense of his plan I go on. "Even with Drakkar dead this is a horrible plan. You're just going to walk in there and ask if Blake is home? It is madness, Alaric."

"He is my brother." The words settle around us in the room.

"I'll go with you." I sigh. "I refuse to let you walk into their den alone. We will go now, with the sunlight as our advantage." I stand from the couch. "Let's get it over with." I turn and head out of the room toward the front door, Alaric follows.

Emily

The dreams torment me. Sebastian, the blade in his hand standing over me as I scream, and no one comes. The darkness taking over my vision as I lay on the bathroom floor. They blur together, one running into the next. I toss and turn. Scream in my sleep. Nothing stops the pain. Nothing blocks the dreams out. The darkness swallows me.

As I resurface from the depths of sleep, I stretch, glad to finally be free of the dreams, of the past and all that it has done to me. I feel him in bed next to me shift, his arms close around me, and I sigh. Snuggling into him further and letting him hold me.

"Hi. How are you feeling?" The deep tenor of his voice vibrates my head sitting on his chest as he shifts me onto him.

"Okay, sore," I admit.

"Yea, you have been out a long time. Six weeks." He doesn't go on.

I slowly open my eyes and the dim light in the room stings them. "I guess that's what happens when you are brought back from the dead." I try to lighten the mood, but feel him tense beneath me and know he is in no mood for it. "Sorry." I clear my throat and look up at him. "I'm starving," I confess as my stomach growls.

"I'll get you something to eat and let Sasha know you're awake. She has been worried sick." I nod and sit up. Stretching my arms over my head and crossing my legs beneath me.

"Tell her to come talk to me, please?" I ask weakly, it has been too long since we spoke. I shut her out just like Theo and I need to see my sister now. I need to talk to her. I need to get it all out.

"She will be glad to hear that. I'm sure she will be in soon. Just relax and take it easy. Don't try to get up yet. You'll be unsteady. I'll help you when I'm back." Theo drops a kiss on the top of my head and leaves the room.

Almost as soon as the door closes it opens again, she must have been waiting on the other side of it for word because Sasha comes rushing into the room with tears in her eyes.

"Big sis!" she squeals as she flies through the air and lands on the bed next to me. The scent of her familiar shampoo fills my nose when she wraps her arms around me.

"I love you, Sash," I tell her, her hair covering my face I take in a deep breath. Grounding myself for the conversation we are about to have. "I'm sorry I shut you out. I'm sorry that I did this. I didn't mean to."

"You don't have to, Em. Theo told us. You don't have to explain. I just want to be here with you. I just want to know I can talk to you and that you're not shutting me out again," she tries to assure me as she pulls back and looks into my eyes.

"I need to get this out. I need to say it out loud to you." I sigh and take a deep breath. "I hurt myself. Again, and again. I needed the pain, needed the rush, the high. It blocked it out. It blocked him out."

"I know, Em. You don't need to apolog—"

"Stop! Let me get this out, Sasha." She looks at me then, the somber look in her eyes changing, she is accepting what I am telling her. I hold my arms out in front of me between us and she looks down at them, I don't miss it when she flinches. "That's not even all of it." I shift in the bed and reveal my lower body to her.

"Emily."

"See, seeing it is different than hearing it from Theo." The wounds have all healed now and all that is left behind is the shiny scars, still pink, I know they will fade in time, but they will forever remain. I will be forever marked by this decision. "I needed to stop seeing Seba—" I clear my throat. "Him." I grind out the word. "I needed to stop seeing him every time I looked at myself in the mirror. I needed to see myself and my choices. I was stupid. I know that now. I took it too far. It was an accident. The cuts kept getting deeper and deeper." I take a long breath before I go on.

"It was an accident." I break and tears slip down my cheeks. "I didn't try to leave you, Sash. I didn't mean to leave you here alone."

"I know. I know you didn't. It is okay." She rubs my knee with her palm, soothing me.

"It isn't, but thank you." I cover her hand with my own. "I promise you I will never do it again. I will never leave you."

Her eyes fill with tears that I don't understand, and I shake my head. "I promise, Sasha, I won't leave you."

She shakes her head. "You will. You will one day, and I will have to watch you grow old and leave me and I will spend an eternity without you." She sobs then, falling forward into my arms. I wrap them around her and brush her hair behind her ear, petting her gently. Trying to ease her mind.

"You won't," I tell her. I know what I am saying. I know the ramifications of what this implies. "You won't have to. I will never leave you again," I swear it to her.

Sasha pulls back and looks up at me. "What are you saying?" She sniffs and wipes her nose with the back of her hand.

"I'm saying what I am saying. I will never leave you." I had a moment of clarity while I dreamt, a moment of truth that I hadn't been able to see before through all of the darkness. It feels as if all the darkness has left my body, bled out with me on the floor in the bathroom and when Theo lifted me from the floor in his arms, I left it all behind. Lighter somehow, my soul light in the darkness of it all.

"Emily?" Sasha starts again.

"I love him. I have loved him. I just haven't been able to let myself feel. I haven't been able to let my walls down. I need time still, but I do love Theo, and I do want to be with him, forever. With you all forever. I want this. I know that now. I know this is my home with you all." I wipe a tear from my cheek and shift uncomfortably on the bed.

"Em," she says my name softly, "I love you."

The door cracks open and Theo sticks his head in. "Am I interrupting?" he asks, pushing the door open a bit further, he has a plate in his hand with some cheese and crackers on it.

"No. You're good." Sasha turns to him and rises from the bed. Sending me a small wave as she leaves the room.

"Come sit down with me." I pat the bed and motion for Theo to come sit with me. I shift on the bed and rest my back on the pillows. He is right. If I tried to get up now, I would hit the floor. I feel weak and tired again.

"You need to eat." He sets the plate down next to me and

then settles himself on the bed.

I pick at the corner of a cracker for a moment. "Theo?" I start. Then think better of it and take a bite from my cracker.

"Just get something in your stomach and we will talk. We have time. You don't need to rush anything." Theo opens his arms to me, and I slide into them, resting on him and setting the plate in my lap. We sit in silence as I eat. But I get full quickly and set the rest on the nightstand for later.

"Theo? I need to tell you something," I pause, "I need you in my life. I need you to ground me. To keep me light, to keep me from the darkness. Not just for those reasons, not because you do those things for me, and I want to use you for it. But I want you. I need you because you complete me. You are my other half. I'm your mate. I love you." I let the last words hang in the air between us. He is still behind me, and I am unable to see his face. Unable to see his eyes.

"What I did was unforgivable. I should never have believed you were capable of hurting me in those ways. Capable of doing those things. I know that. I knew that then. But I was so blinded by fear. Not fear of Se—" I pause, take a deep breath and swallow hard. "Sebastian. Fear of you. Of what loving you meant for me. Of what it meant for us. For the future, for my life. I kept that between us and when everything else went pear-shaped I used it as a weapon against you. I'm sorry for that. It wasn't fair. It was wrong on so many levels and I'm truly sorry. Can you ever forgive me?"

"Emily," Theo starts, then shifts on the bed and pulls me into his lap, facing him. I straddle his hips and stretch my legs out behind him. "I don't need to forgive you for those things. I had done so long ago. I understand, I understood all along. I knew what you were doing, why you were doing it. I just didn't know how to bring you to terms with it on your own. You are my mate, love. You are the one I am meant for. The one I have been searching for for my entire life. I could never dream of not forgiving you. I need to ask you something. I had planned to ask you this regardless if you were ready. I was determined and I have been working out the perfect way to express myself to you. It hasn't worked out. I don't have the perfect thing to say. I don't have all the answers. But I can tell you this, I love you. I have loved you all along and will love you until my last breath, no matter how long from now that is, a hundred years, a thousand, a million. I will love you every day for the rest of my immortal life." Theo kisses me gently on the forehead. "Emily, will you marry me? Be mine? Be my wife? My partner in this life and the next?"

I look into his deep, soulful eyes, smile up at him and kiss him on the cheek. "Of course, I will," I tell him. He kisses me then, soft and filled full of love, of joy. "Theo," I softly say his name as I shift myself in his lap. Brushing against him, the bare skin of my legs wrapped around his waist brush against his hips where his shirt rides up. "Make love to me. Like you did the first time. Like you have wanted to every day since. Show me, show me what it means to be loved by you."

"Emily. You need to rest."

"Don't fight me on this. I am here, begging you for what I need. Don't deny me." I look sadly up at him through my lashes. "Theo," I say his name, putting every ounce of emotion I am feeling into the word.

"Damn it woman," he growls at me.

Slowly he slides his hands up my sides, pushing my shirt up as he goes, exposing my belly and brushing his thumbs over my chilled skin as he does. He lowers his mouth to my neck and kisses me gently, up over my jaw and the side of my face.

"I love you, woman, but you are so damned infuriating at times." I nod, no need to argue a point we both know to be factual. I am aware of the trouble I have caused him, the heartache.

"I love you," I say meekly, hoping to get what I want. I can see the moment he decides. I had a chance, he did consider my request, but I will not win in this, I can see it in his eyes.

"Why don't we get you up and see how you do? Get you a shower and another meal in your belly?" I nod weakly. Defeat filling me. I accept Theo's decision.

"Okay." I scoot backwards out of his lap and turn to the edge of the bed, hanging my feet off it. When the cool floor touches my toes, they tingle.

It feels weird to put weight on my legs. I realize he was right in his denial of me. I am too weak. I have to recover from weeks spent in this bed. Strange how you have to recover from healing.

"Easy," Theo tells me as he helps me to the bathroom, and I shift unsteadily on my feet.

When we enter the bathroom I look down at the tile floor, half expecting it to still be covered in my blood. I look around the room. Taking it all in. It is spotless, there isn't a sign of what happened here left behind. I nod.

"Sit on the edge of the tub for a second, and I'll get the shower started." Theo helps to lower me to the side of the tub. I steady myself with my hands on it and watch as he opens the shower and turns on the water.

Stepping back, he closes the shower door and slips out of his shirt, it falls to the floor between us. Unbuttoning his pants next and pushing them down. I swallow hard as I watch him rise, standing in front of me naked.

"You're killing me," I tell him, nearly eye to eye with his pelvis, I bite my lip.

"Here," he says, holding a hand out to me as he pulls me to him when I rise.

"What are you doing?" I ask, as he slides my shirt off over my head.

"Helping you shower," he says sheepishly, so innocent that I half believe him. I think for a moment he believes himself.

"Mmmhmm. Am I incapable?" I ask, slipping out of my underwear and straightening in front of him.

"No. It is a precaution." I nod at him, a small smile in the corner of my mouth giving me away.

"Mmmhmm," I say again.

We step under the spray of water in the shower, side by side. Theo takes me by the shoulders and turns me in the water, it runs over me and down my back as I look into his eyes.

"Thought you were here to help me shower," I point out when he looks at me with what can only be described as desire of a desperate kind.

"I am." He lifts the shampoo bottle and fills his hand with soap, scrubbing my hair then. I let him massage my scalp. Leaning against his body. My breasts pressed against his chest, my belly brushing against his cock, which despite his insistence on why he is here, tells a different story.

I rinse my own hair, turning to face the wall and letting the soap run down the drain at my feet. When I step back toward Theo, I push my ass against his groin.

"Mmm, Em," he bends and whispers in my ear.

"No, you wanted me to shower and eat," I tease him. Stepping away from him.

The coolness of the bathroom kisses my skin when I step out of the water. Using it to separate us. Theo looks at me, the hurt puppy dog look in his eyes makes me giggle.

"Poor baby. You have to pay for your decisions," I tell

him. Then grab the conditioner and slowly work it through my long hair. Theo sits down on the low bench on the far side of the shower. As I grab a loofa and coat it with body-wash, I lift my leg and rest it on the shower bench behind Theo. Scrubbing the underside of my thigh, dragging it up over my body. Taking my sweet time cleaning myself while he watches. My breasts swing in his face, and he groans.

I stand slowly and repeat the process with the other leg. He keeps his gaze locked on mine this time, refusing to indulge in looking at my naked body, slick with soap. When I step backward into the water, he rises and steps toward me. Catching me off guard. As he reaches for me, I smack his hand away.

"I'm still showering," I scold him like a child.

"Damn my words. Damn what I said. You're a tease."

"Maybe," I confess. "But that isn't my fault. I tried. You said no."

I rinse the conditioner from my hair and the soap from my body. Theo reaches to turn the water off.

"No. You next," I tell him, laughing. Taking joy in teasing this man. My man.

I grab the other loofa and coat it with soap then start to rub it over his chest, down his abdomen, over each arm. I brush my hand against his erection, and he growls at me low in his chest. I make a motion with my finger for him to turn around and he looks up to the ceiling. No doubt praying for strength. I bite my lip, trying to hold back my smile.

"Turn around," I tell him when he doesn't budge. His feet practically glued to the spot. Hands fisted at his sides clench and un-clench.

He does as instructed and turns. I scrub his back slowly, running the loofa over each side of his sculpted ass. Eyeing him as I do. The muscles across his back bunch and I can feel the tension rolling off him. "Perfect," I announce and step back from him. "Now rinse."

Quickly, Theo pushes me to the side and steps into the water, rinsing the soap from his skin in a rush. There are still bubbles clinging to his shoulders when he turns and shuts the water off.

"You missed a spot." I trail my fingers down his back. Goosebumps are left behind in their wake.

"It's fine," he grumbles and steps from the shower. Grabbing a towel and beginning to towel himself dry.

I step out behind him and grab one of my own, wringing out my hair with it and then brushing it over my inflamed skin. The tease is fun, but it is just as much a tease to myself and my belly is filled with a fire of desire and need.

I stroll out of the bathroom past him, dropping the towel on the floor and swinging my hips as I go. Feeling more steady on my feet now, more used to being up and about. I take my time, slowly picking out clothes from the dresser and laying them on the bed. Crossing back and forth from the foot of it to the dresser again and again as Theo stands, towel wrapped around his waist, leaning against the bathroom doorframe watching me.

When I begin to dress, he groans. "Really?"

"Really. You said I needed to eat," I point out, slipping my shirt over my head.

"I'll eat," he murmurs under his breath and steps into the room. Stalking toward me. I'm sure for a moment he will pounce on me. Push me back onto the bed and push himself deep inside me.

Holding my hand out, I press it to his chest. "Get dressed." I point at the pile of clothes I gathered for him, lying next to my pants.

When I bend to pick up the pants and lift a foot into the leg of them, he smacks me on the ass.

"You're going to pay for this." His threat holds a weight to it that leaves me with no doubt I will be paying for this for days once he has his way.

I watch as he quickly dresses, jerking his head into his shirt and pushing his arms aggressively into the sleeves. His pants receive the same assault as he frustratedly puts them on. I cross to the bedroom door, pausing with my hand on the doorknob. When Theo arrives, he rests his hand gently on my back. I turn and lean my body against the length of his, pressing my hips forward into him, I grind against him subtly as I kiss him on the lips hungry and hard. I feel his arms move as he makes to grab me by the waist and I twist away from him, pulling the door open and stepping out into the hall.

I hear him groan behind me and slam his hand on the doorframe. I turn and look at him over my shoulder. Then head for the kitchen.

"Sandwiches?" Theo asks as we enter, starting to pull bread from the shelf.

"Lasagna." I lick my lips. Thinking back to the night we fucked on the kitchen floor then ate lasagna naked.

"That will take hours." Theo turns and stares at me.

"But it is delicious, and you made it for me before. Remember?" I raise an eyebrow, pushing my own memories in my mind to him, willing him to remember that night. Sitting on the kitchen counter making myself come for him. He raises both of his at me in response. Clearly the memories are filling his mind as well.

"Lasagna it is. Whatever you want, Em." I make my way to the large kitchen island and take a seat on a stool as I watch him move his way around the kitchen gathering ingredients.

As time passes, I yawn, feeling sleepy again. Standing and moving over to him on the other side of the counter I slide between his body and the island pressing my own against his.

"Let me help." I start to mix the eggs and cheese together for the filling. Theo's hands take hold of mine, and he moves me about like a puppet as we cook together.

Crossing to the other side of the kitchen he drops the noodles into the now boiling water and then turns back to me. I have perched myself on the kitchen counter. My knees spread wide. My hand resting on my inner thigh suggestively. His eyes go wide, and his mouth thins into a tight line.

"Your water is about to boil over." I point behind him, and he turns back to it. I giggle when he huffs.

"You're a vixen," he tells me as he stirs the pasta.

"I'm just relaxing while you make me dinner." I put my hand to my chest feigning innocence. We both know it is an act. Both know exactly what I am doing.

"Right." He turns and points to a jar of sauce on the counter. "Make yourself useful and open that, spread some in the bottom of the pan over there." His grumpiness makes me smile as I go about the task. I'm glad I'm under his skin. He is under mine. It is only fair.

I turn and look at Theo as he strains the noodles in the colander in the sink. He brings the colander over and sets it onto the counter next to me and we layer the lasagna into the pan. As he pours the last of the sauce over the top of it and sprinkles it with cheese, he puts it in the oven and spins on me.

"We have some time to kill now."

"We need to make a salad," I sputter, nearly laughing out loud as I say the words. Theo glares at me. If looks could kill, I would fall over dead on the kitchen floor.

"The fucking salad can wait. In my bed now, woman." He rushes at me, scoops me up, then carries me from the room.

Chapter 19

EMILY

Theo tosses me backward onto his bed and starts to strip out of his clothes. I watch him, sprawling out on the bed like a cat in the sun. I have no intentions of giving in to him yet.

"You may want to hold off on that, big guy." I stick my toes out at him, pointing at his hand on his jeans button. Theo freezes and looks down at me.

"Emily." The tone of his voice is threatening.

"Theo." I return his name in the same tone. "You said I needed to eat. You said I needed to take it slow."

"You need to take this dick," he blurts out the words, and I die of laughter. Pulling my knees up into my chest and rolling onto my side. "You think that's a joke?"

"I think the lasagna is going to burn if you get those pants off and then I will have nothing to eat." I pout, rolling onto my stomach and resting my chin in the palms of my hands, elbows propped on the bed.

"Goddamnit, woman!" He storms from the room, and I laugh again.

I get up quickly and follow him into the living room.

"Where are you going?"

"To make you a fucking sandwich." He throws the words at me over his shoulder. I laugh again and turn back to the bedroom.

I'm sitting in the middle of the bed naked when he comes back in, legs crossed under me, my hands resting on my thighs.

"What kind of sandwich is it?" I ask sweetly.

"Turkey and cheese." He drops the plate onto the bed next to me. "Eat it." I pick it up and slowly lift it to my mouth. Taking a small bite. As I set the sandwich back down on the plate and chew, Theo sighs and stalks around the room. I slowly lift the sandwich again when he turns and looks at me. Then set it back down and get up from the bed. I go to the bathroom and get a tissue.

Returning, I set it on my knee and settle back onto the bed. "Needed a napkin," I tell him, shrugging.

"Good God, woman." Theo runs his hands through his hair and stalks toward the edge of the bed. I lift the sandwich and take another small bite.

It takes me nearly thirty minutes to eat the thing. I savor every last bite. Then pick at crumbs on the plate. Using my fingertip to pick them up then slowly put it in between my lips and suck the crumbs from it. Theo watches me, eyes slits as he stares me down, still sucking my finger in my mouth. Pushing it in further then sliding it back out with an audible pop.

"Satisfied with yourself?" he asks, clearing his throat.

"Very," I chirp, "it was delicious. Thank you." I smile.

"Is your little game over?" I contemplate his words and

whether or not it is. Whether or not I am done teasing him. This man. My man.

I nod. Theo lunges for me on the bed and I squeal. I fall backward as he collides with me, wrapping his arms around me and pulling me against his chest. His mouth meets mine in a hot, wet kiss. One that is so hungry, it leaves me knowing I pushed him too far. I pushed him to the edge and nearly over it.

His hands run up my sides to my breasts, cupping them, groping them, holding on to me for dear life. His kiss moves over my cheek, down my jaw, and then neck. "I love your big tits, Emily." Theo breaks away from our kiss to tell me. Returning his attention to my mouth he moves over my body, down to my chest, taking a nipple in his mouth he nips at me. Swirling his tongue over the tip of my nipple and making it a peak atop my breast. When he pulls back, he blows on it gently, his warm breath spreading goosebumps over my skin.

Moving to the next he does the same, I gasp when he nips me harder this time. Arching my back and filling his mouth with me. Slowly he moves down over my body, kissing my belly, my hips, trailing his tongue across my skin just above my pubic bone. He reaches my other hip and returns, lowering his mouth to me.

As he closes his mouth over my mound, he slips his tongue down my slit, teasing my clit softly as he brushes against it. His hands continue their motion on my breasts, he massages me, pulls on my nipples, and twists them between his fingers. His mouth continues on my pussy as he slowly trails his fingers down over my body to my hips, then down and over my thighs and venturing back up between my legs.

Slipping a finger inside me he slides it out slowly, then pushes two back into my core. I clamp down around him, embracing the feeling of being filled by him. When Theo rises from me, he takes hold of my wrist and guides my hand to my pussy. "I want to watch you make yourself come," he tells me quietly. Lifting his body from the bed and undressing slowly.

I do as I'm told and circle my clit with my fingers. My eyes never leaving him as he slips out of his clothes and drops them to the floor. When he steps toward me his cock is bobbing in my direction, I bite my lower lip and think about the sensation of having him fill me as I continue my motion on my clit. Think about having him slip inside me and feeling the weight of him on top of me. Theo kneels on the bed and walks his arms up it, one on either side of me.

"Kiss me," I gasp to him. Bringing myself closer to my orgasm.

"Always," he promises and lowers himself over me. His full lips catch mine and our tongues intertwine.

I don't stop. Continuing to rub myself I arch off the bed. "Theo," I gasp his name.

"So soon? You going to come for me, baby?"

I nod emphatically. I'm right there, already feeling the buzz moving over my skin, the tingle in my toes. The jolt of pleasure from my clit shoots through me to my belly and I cry out. He closes his mouth over mine, silencing me as he does. Taking in my gasping breaths as I come beneath him with my hand still on me. I let my fingers go limp. Resting my hand on my inner thigh.

"That won't do," Theo tells me and quickly replaces my fingers with his own on my clit. "Come again for me, baby. I want you begging for me before I'm done with you."

I push myself against the palm of his hand as he slides his fingers down and slips them inside me. Grinding my clit on him wantonly. I need more. He is right, I need so much more. He kisses me gently over my cheeks and then starts his slow path down my body again. His mouth closing over a nipple, long enough for him to nip me before he moves back up to my lips. I get lost in the moment, in his kiss, in the motion of rocking my hips back and forth, rubbing myself on his hand still working my pussy.

"Come for me, Em," he whispers in my ear. "Be a good girl and come for me." The words ignite a fire inside me and the buzz spreads over my skin again. I can feel it building deep inside me. Digging my hands into the sheets I twist them in my fists. Theo coaxes the orgasm out of me with his fingers slowly brushing my inner walls as he palms my clit. I gasp.

"You look so incredible when you come." I barely hear his words as I come, I buck.

Theo moves on the bed, lowering himself over me. As he reaches down and takes hold of the base of his cock, he rubs the head of it up and down my slit. "You're sure you want to marry me. Want to be my wife? There is no going back." His words startle me back into reality.

"Yes. But why are you asking me this now?" I don't understand.

"I'm not going to wait around. I'm not going to lose you. I want you to be my wife. Here. Now." Still confused as to what this has to do with the moment we are in, I nod.

"I'm sure. I want to marry you, Theo."

"Good." Theo pushes forward into me, filling me so suddenly I gasp. Theo stills then, lowering his mouth to mine. He begins to murmur against my lips. "Heart bound to heart, and soul bound to soul." I realize what he was saying, what he is doing. We are doing this, here now. "I am my own, but also yours. Heart bound to heart, and soul to soul bound." He brushes his nose against mine. "One more scar, Em. One to end them all." I nod when he looks deep into my eyes, into my soul. Theo drops his mouth to my neck; I feel his canines brush my skin and when they sink through my flesh I do not scream. I do not fight him. Instead, I fly. "Your turn." He kisses my neck, I can feel the blood trickling down my skin. I know I will be marked by him forever. He has done this before, but without the spell. I remember looking at his mark in the mirror. Deciding not to cover it, to wear it with pride. It is a badge of honor. I am his.

"Heart bound to heart, and soul bound to soul. I am my own, but also yours. Heart bound to heart, and soul to soul bound." I don't hesitate on the words. I speak them clearly, my voice steady. I want this. The magic is heavy in the room around us. It is almost visible in the air.

"I love you," I tell him clearly. "I love you, Theo. Forever bound."

Theo wraps his arms around me and slides into me again, further this time, pushing me open to him. I wrap my legs around his hips and take all of him. We move against each other for a long while, just wrapped in each other's embrace and making love softly. He fills me again and again. I gasp as I get closer to my orgasm and grind my clit against his pelvis. Just as I am about to come, he stills inside me. I whimper out my protest.

"Come here." He slips from my pussy and kneels on the bed, helping me to my hands and knees. Bending over me, he whispers in my ear, "I know what my dirty little slut wants." His words shoot through me to my core, igniting me, waking me from the slow steady pace of our love making and setting me on fire.

I bite my lip, knowing what is coming. When Theo positions himself behind me he rubs me gently with his hand up and down my pussy. Then smacks me on the ass, it is hard and the reverberations of it leave me shaking. My skin stings, he does it again, and again. I'm panting, the pain is bringing me so close to the edge of coming that I can't think straight.

Suddenly he shoves forward into me, impaling me with

his hard cock. I gasp and explode around him. Clenching down around him as he fills me further.

"You want me to fuck you like a good little whore?" he asks, I nod. He knows me. He knows what I like. I wanted him to make love to me soft and sweet, but this is what I need. This is what lights me on fire from the inside out.

"Yes. Fuck me, Theo." I growl the words at him, sounding more animal than human.

"Mmmhmm." He pounds into me, then stills, reaching down and taking me by the wrists. I arch my back and steady myself on my knees, my arms pulled behind my back.

Theo uses his grip on me to pull me further back onto him. When he releases me and pushes in the center of my back between my shoulder blades I fall forward onto the bed. He plants his foot on the bed next to me and uses the new position to pin me down, his hand on my back. He is rough with me then and I go wild over it.

Theo pounds into me, the sound of our bodies colliding together fills the room. Our pants coming out in unison. Suddenly he stops, switching up positions again and taking me by a hand fisted in my hair. "On your knees." He pulls me to the edge of the bed, then lets me settle onto my knees next to it. I look up at the man holding my head steady in his hand as he looks down at me, his treatment of my body everything I crave, but the love in his eyes makes my heart explode.

"Open that pretty little mouth. You thought you could get away with being sassy, with teasing me and leading me on? I told you that you would pay for it." He runs his fingers down over my jaw and chin tipping my face up toward him as I part my lips.

When he slides the head of his cock between my lips the taste of myself on his skin coats my tongue. I swirl it around him, letting him push into the back of my throat. I reach a hand up and cup his balls, watching Theo toss his head back and feeling his grip on my hair tighten. I play with his balls, pulling and twisting them gently as he uses my mouth and fucks my face.

"God, you're a good little cocksucker," he tells me, and I smile around him.

This dominant darker side of him I had been asking him for before is shaking me to my core and I can feel the orgasm building just from pleasing him. Theo uses his free hand to reach down and twists my nipple in his fingers. The pleasure pain shoots through my core to my clit as I sit back on my legs and grind myself against them. Squeezing my thighs together against the sensations growing between them.

"Good girl, make yourself come for me while you suck my cock." I nod and continue doing as I'm told.

The buzzing moving over my skin brings me to life and I start to buck. As my ecstasy flows through me I squeeze my eyes closed and see stars on my eyelids.

"Look at me," Theo commands. His voice is hoarse, and I can tell he is holding back his own climax.

Our eyes meet and his flash with something I don't understand. Something is there that he hasn't told me, something that he is debating in his mind. I can see it written all over his face. I still and then pull back from him as he releases my head.

"What? What aren't you saying?" The fun of the moment is lost, and I have an uneasy feeling growing inside me, a lump lodging in my throat.

Theo holds his arms out to me, and I stand, unsteady on my feet for a moment. He sits me down on the edge of the bed and settles between my legs on his knees, cupping my cheek in his hand. "The spell isn't complete, and I want you to make the decision. I won't make it for you." Looking back and forth between his eyes I wonder what this means for me, for us. "You are my mate. It is a mating, Emily." The words settle around me, the weight of them sinking in.

I lay back on the bed, swinging my legs around and positioning myself in the middle of it. Staring up at the ceiling, hands folded over my belly. Theo stretches out on his back next to me. "So, you mean?" I start, then stop myself. I think it through. It doesn't take me more than a moment. I know the truth in my heart. I know what I want. I love this man. After everything that we have been through, all that he has done for me, I know what is right.

Slowly I roll onto my side, planting my hand for leverage and swing a leg over Theo's hips. I position myself over top of him, lowering myself onto his still erect cock. I toss my head back at the feeling of being so full. Remembering the night I rode him in my kitchen before we ate lasagna together in the dim light of the night.

I ride him slowly at first, then we find our pace, Theo places his hands on my hips and pushes me down against his body. Filling me, grinding my clit against him. I toss my head back and moan.

"Fuck, yes," I call into the night.

"That's right. You love this cock, don't you?" He teases my nipples with his fingers as he asks me the question. They feel like they're connected to my pussy, a direct line to my clit, each time he pinches and twists I feel the jolt of pleasure between my legs.

I ride him harder, faster, and smile when he bucks beneath me. Lifting his hips to fill me more. I tense down around him, trying to draw him deeper into me. I need the friction, need the depth, need to have every part of me filled with him. Claiming me as his. Losing track of where I stop, and he begins.

"I'm going to come, Emily. I'm going to fill you with it and make you mine." The words send goosebumps over my skin, my scalp tingles. I want to be his, I want to be claimed, to be marked, to be owned by this man for an eternity. I keep my steady pace, refusing to turn back now. "Come for me. Come with me. I want to feel you come around me while I fill you. I want to watch the look in your eyes when you come apart at the seams from having me inside you."

I lean over him, placing my hands on either side of his head and letting my breasts swing in front of his face. He nips at them, and I bite my lower lip, holding back my cry when he catches a nipple between his teeth and then swirls his tongue over the tip of it. I rock back on my heels, pressure of my nipple still caught between his teeth pulls and fills me with the pleasure pain that throws me into the abyss.

Theo meets me there and I can feel him swell inside me, he bucks beneath me filling me with his come, until at last we are both twitching with jolts of aftershocks. I fall forward onto his chest just as his arms come around me and hold me close to him.

"I love you." Theo's murmured words fill me with joy, and I sleepily close my eyes, resting my head on his shoulder.

"I love you, too," I tell him gently.

A short while later my stomach growls and he looks down at me. "Lasagna?"

"Lasagna," I agree.

We slip from the bedroom in the darkness and head to the kitchen, standing at the island in just his oversized t-shirt I eat my lasagna and look into the eyes of the man I love, the man who has done so much for me, the man I am meant to be with for an eternity.

Epilogue

Theo

Alaric and I have been waiting in the lobby of the tattoo studio for hours. Sasha checks in with us periodically letting us know that progress is coming along, and we have to be patient. I bounce my knee. Anxious for what is coming, anxious for Emily's big reveal. As the minutes tick by I finally stand and pace the room.

We discussed this at length, I know what to expect and this is no shock to me that Emily has decided to do this, but the waiting is killing me. "I'm going to get a cup of coffee," I tell Alaric and storm from the studio. The air outside fills my lungs and helps to ease my mind. I know no one is hurting her. I know that. But I know she is enduring a pain to cover the past, to cover a pain she endured because of me and my failure to protect her.

I walk along the sidewalk of the shopping center and into the coffee shop, waiting in line for my turn and place my order. In the back of my mind, I know the caffeine will be unhelpful with my nerves. But I needed something to do with myself. I walk around the rest of the center and sip my coffee. Thinking through our plans for the rest of the day, trying to distract my mind. When I hear my name from behind me, I turn and see Sasha standing on the sidewalk out front of the tattoo studio.

I toss my cup in the nearest trashcan and jog down the sidewalk toward Sasha. "Is she done?"

"Done!" Sasha beams at me and I know that is a good sign. "She is finishing up getting dressed right now. She wants you to go home." I gawk at her.

"What? Why?" I try to pass her on the sidewalk and get to the door of the studio.

"She wants to show you as a whole, at home, not here where you can only see a portion of it. She wants to meet you at home. Go home," Sasha demands, my eyes go wide and for a minute I think she is going to stamp her foot at me.

"Fine." I turn and head to the truck.

Fuming the entire way home. I understand her reasoning behind it. But still my impatience is killing me. I head to the kitchen and busy myself in there. Before long I hear the front door open, and voices fill the house as Alaric, Sasha, and Emily return home. Alaric appears in the doorway of the kitchen with a massive grin on his face.

"You've seen it?" I rush toward him.

"Not all of it. That is only for you." His grin spreads.

Quickly I leave the kitchen and my brother behind. I pass Sasha in the living room. "She is ready for you." She smiles at me, and I don't even pause to look at her.

I get to the bedroom door and stop, with my hand on the doorknob. Taking in a deep breath to steady myself, I turn the knob and push the door open. Emily is standing naked in the middle of the room with her back to me. She is gorgeous and I need to see the rest of her, I need her to turn toward me.

"Em?" I step slowly toward her, closing the door behind me.

When she turns and looks at me, I gasp, I can't take it all in at first. I pause and look her up and down. Across her temple, down the side of her face, and over her collarbone I focus my vision first. The tiny blue starbursts scattered over her skin, encircle the scars there, covering, twirling around, trailing along them. My eyes hitch at her breasts for a moment then continue along the path down her rib cage to her hips, swirls of stars cover her skin and scars, wrapping around to her inner thighs. Emily takes a step toward me and holds out her arms to me, the stars cover her there too, up from the deepest of her scars on her wrists, from the morning I simply cannot forget, all the way to her elbows.

She is a constellation in the darkness of the room. She glows with the beauty of it. My Emily, my very own Cassiopeia, Queen of the stars, my mate. Her beauty is astounding and when she smiles at me, the biggest smile I have ever seen on her face, I know she feels the same, I know she will be able to look at herself and love what she sees now. Love her reflection again just as much as she has worked to love herself over the past few months.

"Emily," I call her name and as she moves toward me, she almost shimmers in the dim light of the room.

"Make love to me, Theo." The words fill my heart and I know she is thinking back to the first day we were here together, the first time, and every other after that. For an eternity, she will forever be my fallen star that has risen again.

Emmy Lou Hayes

Emmy Lou Hayes is a married mother of three. Originally from Ohio, she has lived the majority of her life in Maryland. While attending college she worked at a local sandwich shop, where she met her husband. When not working or at home in Southern Maryland, they enjoy spending time traveling the country in their RV with their children and two dogs. Emmy Lou works full time in the Medical field, but her passion is writing and sharing that writing with others. With an affinity for erotica and BDSM, Emmy Lou hopes to keep her readers coming back for more again and again.

Visit her website here:
http://emmylouhayes.com/

Don't miss these exciting titles by Emmy Lou Hayes and Blushing Books!

Marked
Branded
Scarred

Her Unexpected Mate series
The Alpha's Melody
Second Chance Summer
For the Love of Sam
A Shift in Ciara
Broken Rae of Light

His Submissive
The Release
The Capture

Blushing Books

Blushing Books is one of the oldest eBook publishers on the web. We've been running websites that publish spanking and BDSM related romance and erotica since 1999, and we have been selling eBooks since 2003. We hope you'll check out our hundreds of offerings at http://www.blushingbooks.com.

Blushing Books Newsletter

Please join the Blushing Books newsletter
to receive updates & special promotional offers.
You can also join by using your mobile phone:
Just text BLUSHING to 22828.